LUCY BRANDT

LEONORA BOLT

THE GREAT GADGET GAMES

PUFFIN

PUFFIN BOOKS

UK | USA | Canada | Ireland | Australia
India | New Zealand | South Africa

Puffin Books is part of the Penguin Random House group of companies
whose addresses can be found at global.penguinrandomhouse.com.

www.penguin.co.uk
www.puffin.co.uk
www.ladybird.co.uk

Penguin
Random House
UK

First published 2023

001

Text design by Nigel Baines
Printed in Great Britain by Clays Ltd, Elcograf S.p.A.

The authorized representative in the EEA is Penguin Random House Ireland,
Morrison Chambers, 32 Nassau Street, Dublin D02 YH68

A CIP catalogue record for this book is available from the British Library

ISBN: 978–0–241–62210–0

All correspondence to:
Puffin Books
Penguin Random House Children's
One Embassy Gardens, 8 Viaduct Gardens, London SW11 7BW

For Dan, Dave, Liz, Mac and Jude

Contents

1	A Proper Turkey	1
2	On Your Marks	13
3	All Spruced Up	26
4	Spaniel Fir	34
5	Card Games	43
6	Identigo	51
7	Get Set	63
	Chapter 7 *and a Smidge*	73
8	We Love You, Luther	76
9	Get Ready	86
10	In the Pines	95

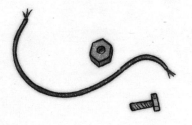

11	Teamwork Makes the Dream Work	109
12	Perfect Dismount	121
13	Checkpoint Checkmate	132
	Chapter 13 *and 3 Ounces*	141
14	The Blunder Bureau	145
15	The Department of Whoops	156
16	Showtime	166
17	Family Misfortunes	173
18	Backstage Passes	186
19	Father's Day	198

1
A Proper Turkey

Just because you *can* invent something, it really doesn't mean that you *should*.

Take bungee jumping, for example. Daredevil grown-ups think it's a terrific idea to strap big rubber bands to their legs and hurl themselves face-first off cliffs, bridges and other incredibly tall things. It's basically a triumph of elastic over extreme silliness.

And what about chutney? Which genius decided that vegetables would taste *better* stuffed in jars of vinegar and left at the back of kitchen cupboards for about three hundred years? The grim brown chunks then spread over perfectly innocent sandwiches.

As you can see, not all human invention is impressive. Many of our biggest brainwaves are more like brain-blurps.

Leonora Bolt was pondering the world of ridiculous ideas on this her first proper Christmas morning. Relaxing in the living room of her lighthouse home, she was trying hard to understand why anyone would hide teeth-shattering silver trinkets inside a pudding, then serve it *on fire*. Or cover their house in baubles, greenery and glitter so that it resembles a spangle-tastic shrubbery. Or eat bad mince pies.

'Do you likes them?' asked Mildred, one of Leonora's guardians. She was looming over her with a plate of festive pastries, an eager look on her face.

Leonora took another cautious bite, the soft, buttery pastry giving way to – **URGH!** What was that? Some sort of gritty raisin sludge? It was so sweet that it made Leonora's cheeks vibrate.

'Hmmm . . . yum,' she replied, feeling dried fruit weld itself to the roof of her mouth. 'Why do we eat these again?'

'Well, they're *traditional*,' said Mildred.

They're criminal more like, thought Leonora. As Mildred turned and bustled about the room once more, Leonora quietly yacked her mouthful into a Santa napkin.

'And it's important you learn about all the festive traditions,' Mildred continued, handing her a glass of mulled plum juice and smiling to reveal teeth like a pirate's. 'After all, you've got some catching up to do.'

Leonora took the warm cinnamon-scented squash and grinned right back. This year Mildred had gone into overdrive to make up for all the Christmases that Leonora had missed. Which were an awful lot.

That's because up until now, her ghastly Uncle Luther had banned them. He'd also

4

forbidden laughing, skipping, cartoons, games, cuddles, dancing and pretty much all other happy activities. He sounds horrible, right? Well, let me tell you that whatever sort of man you're imagining, he was LOADS MORE dreadful than that. You see, Uncle Luther had adopted Leonora when she was just three years old and raised her on the tiny but magical wilderness of Crabby Island. It was a place of waves and heathered rock, mysterious coves and creeping tides, far, far away from the mainland.

Uncle Luther had realized early on that Leonora was a total flipping genius who adored inventing. Incredible ideas glugged out of her brain like a leaky tap (often causing a tidal wave of trouble). And because he was a failed professor with no real talent of his own, he saw his chance to snaffle hers and make his fortune.

Instead of sending her to school, he made Leonora spend all day alone in a workshop at the top of the lighthouse. There she created astounding gadgets like **turbo toothbrushes**, **nose cosies** and **remote-controlled geese**. Uncle 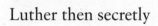 Luther then secretly *stole* her ideas and sold them on the mainland, becoming wealthy and famous. And since he never let her leave Crabby Island, always pretending that he was too busy with his work to take her, she had no idea about his double life, or the success of her brilliant inventions.

Like a real-life Grinch, Uncle Luther had also stolen Christmas from Leonora. Before this week, she couldn't remember decking the halls with boughs of holly or opening a stocking full of presents. And she'd never experienced the joy of stomping through a hot shopping centre in search of a fake Santa's grotto. (Perhaps some things about her childhood hadn't been *all* bad.)

But worse than stealing her ideas, and even more mean than keeping Christmas from her, Uncle Luther had also taken Leonora's genius parents prisoner, forcing them to work on devious schemes for his company, Brightspark Industries. And he'd told Leonora that she was an orphan.

But the truth, like toothpaste (truthpaste?), always gets squeezed out in the end. Leonora had recently discovered that her parents were 100 per cent alive! And she was 1,000,000,000 per cent determined to get them back.*

---

* You can't really have 1,000,000,000 per cent, so please don't tell your teacher about my made-up maths.

Leonora had scored a hat-trick when it came to ruining Uncle Luther's evil plans.

Goal number one: she'd stopped him entering the Society of Ingenious Geniuses (known as **SIG** for short) – a top-secret organization of amazing inventors. Leonora's parents and Mildred had all worked there as super scientists, and Uncle Luther had tried to join too so that he could run off with a powerful emotion-controlling formula.

Goal two: Leonora had built a wonky submarine and sailed it to the ocean depths to destroy her uncle's happiness-stealing machine.

Goal three: she'd crossed the Perilous Desert in a grumpy robotic camel, shut *down the eco-disaster BrightWorld theme park, and stopped Luther from brainwashing the world's children into feeling numb to joy.*

Despite all this, Leonora hadn't yet won the match. Uncle Luther was always one step ahead of her, and he still had her parents hidden away. But she vowed that she'd never stop, never give up, and that she'd move heaven and earth to rescue them next time.

'Don't you be worrying,' said Mildred, as if reading her thoughts. 'It'll be the last Christmas we spend apart from Eliza and Harry, I promise you that.'

'I'm sure it will, Millie –' Leonora gave a determined nod – 'and this is still a brilliant Christmas, thank you.'

Leonora pushed away all thoughts of her mum and dad locked up in a miserable prison somewhere. Instead, she focused on the clues that they'd hidden for her back at the theme park. The number 313 was important somehow, and so was the phrase 'a world turned upside down'. Leonora also knew that her parents had made a big scientific discovery aboard a boat called HMS *Invisible* six years before. That was when Uncle Luther had kidnapped them. What had they found? Why was it so important?

Leonora took out a pocket notebook and pencil. She scribbled a quick to-do list:

Work out the '313' and 'a world turned upside down' clues.

Find HMS Invisible.

Rescue Mum and Dad!

It took much less time to write down her to-don't list:

DO NOT *fail this time!*

'Och, sorry I musta dozed off,' came a gentle voice beside her. It was Leonora's other guardian – hapless ocean explorer and song botherer Captain Spang.

'Are ye having a happy day, wee lassie?' he asked, sitting up in his rocking chair, bangles jangling. Leonora's pet otter, Twitchy Nibbles, woke up too. He yawned, stretched and performed a roly-poly on the rug next to her.

Leonora nodded, smiling at them both. She snuggled her face into Twitchy's warm chestnut fur. Outside the lighthouse, they could see snowflakes drift down from a gunmetal-grey sky. Inside, the air was sweet with the smell of pine and spices. All was calm. All was bright. A sense of peace seemed to fill the little room and also fill Leonora's heart.

But about thirty seconds later, all that lovely

calmness was smashed to smithereens. There came a sudden jingling, jangling noise from far below, like a thousand sleigh bells on the blink. It was mixed with tinny singing so aggressively cheerful that it could wake the Christmas spirits (and make them want to bury themselves all over again):

'DING-DONG MERRILY ON HIGH!!!!'

2

On Your Marks

'What was that?' cried Leonora, her heart skidding to a halt.

'The postman?' replied Mildred warily.

'Carol singers?' offered Captain Spang.

'We don't get post –' Leonora jumped up with Twitchy and dashed over to the windows – 'and our nearest neighbours are over seventy kilometres away, by boat.'

Leonora rubbed a circle on the misty glass with her palm and scanned the horizon. She felt a bit sick (only partly because she'd scoffed an entire tin of Toffee Apocalypse truffles for breakfast). Had Uncle Luther broken through

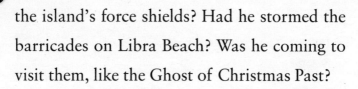

the island's force shields? Had he stormed the barricades on Libra Beach? Was he coming to visit them, like the Ghost of Christmas Past?

'I – I can't see anything,' she said, searching in all directions. 'And, look –' Leonora pulled a device from her dungaree pocket and tapped the screen – 'there's no reading on my **Bad Uncle Monitor** either.' Twitchy pressed his wet nose against the window and stared out too, whiskers primed for peril.

'Panic over! I thinks I knows who it is,' said Mildred. She pointed towards a blonde head just visible through the snow several storeys below.

'Oh, phew, it's only Jack.' Leonora felt a rush of relief. 'That's weird, I didn't think he could come today. I'd better go and let him in.'

Less than two minutes later, Leonora and Twitchy had whizzed down the banister of their spiral staircase and bounded out of the front door. She was now happily smooshing a welcome snowball into Jack's face.

He laughed, batting her away with his spare hand. 'Urk, Merry Chrimble to you too! Now get off!'

'**SQUOOKY-SQUOOK!**' called Twitchy, hopping in giddy circles round Jack's legs.

Jack was Leonora's very bestest best friend. Technically he was her *only* friend, given that she'd grown up alone except for Mildred, Twitchy and her uncle. He lived in the boring village of Snorebury-on-Sea, on the mainland, with his mum, dad and ten siblings. He had a heart of solid gold (not literally – that would be heavy) and he'd been Leonora's loyal companion on all her adventures.

'I thought you couldn't make it,' said Leonora, laying off her attack. 'Won't your family notice you're missing on Christmas Day?'

'Nah, it's OK. Mum, Jim, Jessica, Juliet, Jonny, Joseph, Joel and Jasmine are stuck in a never-ending game of reindeer roulette. Josie and Jake are arguing over a snow-fairy outfit. And Dad's hiding in the kitchen with baby Dennis, peeling about a bajillion sprouts. No one will realize I've snuck out.'

'OK, cool,' she said. 'Did you park the car in our secret place?'

'Of course I did,' he replied, waving vaguely over his shoulder towards Libra Beach. Leonora could just about see the gold Rolls-Royce in the bay far below. It was the amazing land-sea car that they'd used to escape from Uncle Luther's underwater lair.

'And did you reset the **WIFS**?'

'Yep, the Whole Island Force Shield is back on. I'm not a numpty,' he said, rolling his eyes.

'Not a *complete* one,' she said, grinning at Jack's garish festive jumper. 'Only like ninety-nine per cent, wearing that.'

'Shut up, it's traditional,' he said, laughing.

Jack made his way into the lighthouse as Leonora took one last look towards the murky horizon. Uncle Luther had a horrible habit of appearing out of nowhere, but this time the coast seemed to be clear.

'Happy Christmas and come on in!' cried Mildred, as they entered the living room a few moments later. She managed to ruffle Jack's hair and shove a slab of fruitcake into his mouth in one smooth movement.

'Aye, season's greetings, young man!' said Captain Spang, playing a little ditty on the piccolo and cymbals.

'Hwappee Cwithmuth, bleverywun,' replied Jack, spraying out sultanas.

While Jack tackled the cake, Leonora rushed over to the Christmas tree and rummaged underneath. She pulled out several mysterious parcels, an excited gleam in her eye. 'Homemade presents!' she announced. 'A load of new stuff washed up on Phoenix Beach last week, so I recycled it.'

'Ma proper eco-engineer,' said Captain Spang with a proud nod.

'Here, this is for you.' She handed a gift to Jack.

'Wow, it's . . . just what I've always wanted,' he said, unwrapping a white leathery lump. 'Um, what is it?'

'It's a **Sure-Shot**,' she said, 'a laser-guided football that never misses the goal. And this is for you, Millie,' she said, watching as Mildred unwrapped a long, thin package. 'It's a rocket-propelled whisk to make mixing easier.'

'Oh, you are clever; I loves it!' cried Mildred.

One by one they all exchanged their homemade gifts. Mildred gave them boiled-cabbage candy canes. Captain Spang sang an incredibly long carol about elves. Twitchy dropped shiny pebbles at their feet, nudging a heart-shaped one towards Leonora and gazing at her with eyes like melted chocolate. Leonora felt her chest squeeze with happiness. She fished out five otter leg-and-tail warmers. 'Happy Chrimble, Twitch,' she said, hugging him tightly.

'Here, got this for you,' said Jack at last, handing Leonora a gift. 'Sorry it's not much. I don't get pocket money.'

'Hey, I didn't want you to spend anything,' said Leonora. 'Just you being here is . . . ahh . . . like a present,' she mumbled, before punching him on the arm. She unwrapped Jack's parcel to reveal a small red tube.

'Micro fire extinguisher. Fits in your pocket,' he said. 'Thought it might come in handy the next time you explode something.'

'Hey! It's been a whole two days since I did that!' Leonora cried in mock outrage. 'But thanks – we might need it for the Christmas crackers later. I made the snaps using new **Kaboom 'n' Fly** extra-strength dynamite.'

'Oh . . . *fantastic*,' said Jack.

Twitchy groaned.

'Och, what was the music we heard when you arrived, Jack me lad?' asked Captain Spang. 'It sounded cheery.'

'Oh yeah, I nearly forgot. This arrived through our letterbox today.' Jack pulled a crumpled Christmas card from his back pocket and handed it to Leonora. On the front was a gold star with *Great Gadget Games* underneath.

As she opened it, the music blasted out again:

'DING-DONG MERRILY ON HIGH!!!!'

'Ooof! My ears!' Leonora shouted above the jingling. She slammed it shut. 'Who sent you that?'

'No idea, but everyone in the village got one. Thought you might like to see it, as I know you don't get post here.'

Leonora rubbed her forehead. She cracked the card open a bit. Inside it was blank except for three words: *On Your Marks . . .*

'What do you thinks it means?' asked Mildred.

'Probably just a joke,' said Jack, shrugging.

'Yeah . . . maybe.' Leonora popped the card on the mantlepiece and soon forgot about it as they prepared the Christmas dinner.

Since Mildred had rejoined SIG as a top food scientist, her cooking had taken a turn for the better. Leonora calculated that 53 per cent of it was now fit to be eaten by humans, and only 22 per cent was likely to cause some kind of public health emergency. Mildred had even started using exciting new ingredients, like 'sugar'.

They ran up and down from the lighthouse kitchen, carrying plates piled with honey-glazed carrots and roast spuds, pink hams and spiced buns. At one point Leonora nearly dropped a bowl of treacle twirls, skidding on some stray baubles and pine needles that were scattered across the floor. And over the course of the afternoon they ate like royals (although everyone passed on the mistle toast and ivy gravy). As night's inky fingertips crept across the sky, with bellies full and hearts content, they settled down in front of the TV.

'Let me see if I can get it started,' said Leonora, cranking a handle on the side of her recycled TV set like a jack-in-the-box. The screen flickered on, showing grainy black-and-white pictures as if beaming in from 1960. Leonora had never had to sit through festive programmes before. And unfortunately for her, they were broadcasting a Christmas special that was anything but.

It was *The Late Daily Tonight* Show with host Barry Tremendous and celebrity guest . . . Luther Brightspark.

3
All Spruced Up

'Thank you for having me, Barry,' Uncle Luther was saying from his spot on the chat-show sofa. 'And what a *marvellous* crowd you have in tonight.' The audience clapped and cheered.

Leonora felt all the festive loveliness disappear. Her skin crawled as if she was suddenly covered in invisible ants. Despite this, she couldn't help noticing that Uncle Luther didn't look his usual smart self. He was wearing a shabby suit and had stubble on his chin.

'Now, Luther, tell us all about your latest grand plans,' said Barry in a voice so slick it could practically oil the wheels of a train.

'Well, Barry, I'm here to announce something very special.' Luther didn't sound excited at all. 'The Great Gadget Games. It's a global inventing competition for children.'

'The bare-faced cheek of the man!' cried Mildred, glaring at the screen. 'He shouldn't be on a chat show; he should be in a prison!'

'Aye, he's as guilty as a ship's cat in the galley!' agreed Captain Spang.

Leonora wasn't exactly sure what the Captain meant, but she was just as upset as her guardians to see Luther on TV. 'Shhh, I can't hear him.' Leonora shuffled nearer to the screen. She willed the shaky picture not to cut out.

Uncle Luther was continuing: 'I've sent a Christmas card to every household in the world. Your first test is to work out how to use the invitation to enter the games. Only the brightest sparks will be able to solve *that* little puzzle. Succeed, and you'll get to take part in

28

the greatest celebration of inventing ever seen!'

Leonora stared in disbelief at her awful uncle. *Parent-kidnapper and shameless crook!* He lied as easily as breathing and his crimes got more daring every time. And yet here he was being worshipped on television as if he'd done *nothing* wrong at all.

'But what about your mishap in the desert?' asked Barry. 'There were more than a few disappointed customers after your BrightWorld theme park failed to open. And wasn't there a row with the locals in Balmy about you taking their water supply?'

For a split second Leonora saw telltale rage roll across her uncle's face. If looks could kill, Barry would've been halfway to hell. But Uncle Luther swiftly calmed himself again and spoke directly to the camera.

'Ah yes, unfortunately my theme park was ruined by a team of jealous hooligans. But

Brightspark Industries is back, and better than ever. The victor of the Great Gadget Games will become an apprentice at my company, and win an exclusive jewel-encrusted . . . *me*!'

A model of Uncle Luther flashed on screen, studded with diamonds, emeralds and rubies. There were gasps from the studio audience.

'And the most exciting part is that I've persuaded a couple of top boffins to judge the winner of the final round on New Year's Eve. None other than superstar scientists Eliza and Harry Bolt!'

Eliza and Harry Bolt

Leonora felt as if all the oxygen had left the room. *Mum and Dad!*

'This *is* a big surprise!' It was Barry's turn to lose his cool. 'Weren't Eliza and Harry reported . . . erm . . . *missing* a few years back?'

'Pish and piddle,' said Uncle Luther. 'Those cheeky rascals have been living in secluded luxury in Monte Fantastico. I practically had to beg them to leave their sunloungers.'

'That's a load of old rubbish!' cried Jack.

'He's totally lost it this time,' agreed Mildred. 'The cheese has come right off his crackers!'

'Super!' said Barry. He then turned to address the viewers at home. 'Well, that's all we have time for tonight, folks. You kids have until midnight to apply for the Great Gadget Games. Best of luck, everyone!'

With that, the audience burst into applause, the lights darkened and Leonora's tatty TV conked out.

No one said anything for a very long time. The fire grumbled in the grate. Leonora eventually stood up and started to pace the room. A million thoughts were hurtling through her mind, as if they were trying to win a relay race. 'Well, there's nothing for it,' she said at last, swiping the card from the mantlepiece. 'I've just got to enter the games!'

Twitchy hopped over and clamped himself to her ankle as if to say, 'NO WAY!'

'It's a trap!' said Mildred. 'I can't risk him taking you again.'

'Yeah,' agreed Jack, 'it's a really bad idea. Worse than that time you tried to sail a concrete canoe.'

Leonora paused, looking from Mildred to Jack to Captain Spang. She felt fear prickle her scalp as she remembered Uncle Luther almost capturing her in his deep-sea lair, and again at BrightWorld. It was stupidly dangerous to apply for the games, and yet . . . what choice did she have? She couldn't let Uncle Luther parade her parents like puppets on TV. Or make himself even richer and more popular by stealing new ideas for gadgets from children everywhere. No, it was down to her to save her mum and dad and expose Luther's lies to the world once and for all!

'I know it's risky, but I'll invent a really clever disguise,' she said, slapping a fist into her palm, 'and it'll be the best one *ever*.'

'Perhaps I can help with that,' came a posh voice from out of nowhere.

Everyone jumped and stared wildly about the room. It took Leonora several moments to realize what was happening. And when she did she was sure that the cheese had come off her crackers too.

The Christmas tree had started talking.

4
Spaniel Fir

'It's all right! I won't bite,' said the tree, waving a middle branch, which just added to the terrifying effect.

Leonora felt a wave of giddiness. *I'm in shock from seeing Uncle Luther on TV. And eating too many truffles! This is a sugar-based delusion – no need to panic!*

Jack, on the other hand, was doing all the panicking for her. 'Show yourself, you – you coward!' he cried, seizing the moment and the scariest weapon to hand (a chocolate trifle).

'Aye, come out you, er, cowardy custard!' added Captain Spang. Twitchy hissed and hopped about, as if fancy footwork could bamboozle the frightening fir.

As they backed towards the door, the tree stopped waving and started to shake, rattle and roll instead. There was a humming noise like a swarm of disgruntled bees arguing over directions. And before their eyes the tree turned into –

'Brenda! What the fiddly flipcakes are you doing here?' cried Mildred.

Before them stood Brenda Spaniel from SIG. The Diva of Disguise. The Queen of Costume. The Empress of Outfits. She was wearing her usual tweed suit, looking just as she did when she had helped Leonora destroy Uncle Luther's underwater lair.

'Happy Christmas, one and all!' she said, grabbing a glass of plum juice. 'I imagine you have a few questions.'

'Yeah, just one or two,' said Jack.

'What the – what just *happened*?' said Leonora, rushing over and examining Brenda and the space around her, where just moments before there had been a jolly tree. Twitchy, meanwhile, had gathered up all the shiny pebbles and was guarding them with a ferocious look.

'Give Brenda room to breathe,' said Mildred, ushering her towards an armchair. 'I'm sure she has a simple explanation.'

'Hmmm, bet she doesn't,' said Jack.

'Aye, that was quite an entrance,' said Captain Spang. 'Proper theatrics!'

'Yeah,' said Leonora, 'but sorry about jamming that fairy on your head this morning.'

'Ah, I wasn't here at that point,' said Brenda. 'I hid in the car boot when Jack sailed over, and adopted my disguise while you were all bringing lunch up from the kitchen. Apologies, I threw your actual tree out of the window. Great decoration job, though, given it was your first time.' Brenda gave Leonora a sympathetic look.

Leonora stared back. Not in a million, basquillion years would she have guessed that their Christmas tree was, in fact, former village busybody Brenda. She peered around the room, wondering what other ordinary household items might be about to take human form.

'Anyway, I'm here to tell you that, since your desert escapade, Luther has recruited more spies than ever,' Brenda went on. 'You need to tighten up island security. Expect the unexpected. As you can see, I've been busy developing this new shape-shifting technology at SIG.'

Leonora's brain raced to the finishing line. 'Could I use it to enter the Gadget Games?' she asked.

'Ah . . . possibly,' said Brenda, sipping her drink. 'So far, I've mostly managed to transform myself into greenery, not people.'

'So Leo could compete, but only disguised as a pot plant?' Jack hid a snigger behind his hand.

'Indeed. And I'm sorry to interrupt your festivities,' continued Brenda, 'but, Leonora, you must come to SIG headquarters right now and help us fine-tune the technology. That way you might have a chance to enter the games undetected.'

Leonora nodded. 'OK. And is there any news about the clues from my parents we found in the desert? The number "313", the phrase "a world turned upside down", and the boat, HMS *Invisible?*'

'We have our very best team working round the clock to solve those riddles,' said Brenda. 'After your parents were kidnapped from the ship by Luther, it sailed back to Port Mystery. We're trying to track its whereabouts now.'

'But are you sure I'm allowed back at SIG?' Leonora asked, trying to keep the sulky edge from her voice. 'Professor Insignia was clear that it's not a place for children.'

'Insignia has some old-fashioned views,' muttered Mildred, 'but he believes he's doing the right thing.'

Leonora sighed. 'Right, so all we have to do

is work out how to enter the games and make me a foolproof disguise – all by midnight?'

Brenda nodded. 'We know it's a tall order, but Luther must be stopped. Your triumph over his evil plans in the desert put a large dent in his finances and his popularity. He'll be desperate to use the games as a means to claw back both.'

'And do you think Mum and Dad will really be there this time?'

Brenda lowered her voice. 'According to our SIG spy network, yes, we do. We believe that they're being taken to a secret TV studio ahead of the final. We'll try to rescue them before they get there and bring this whole charade to a stop, but security will be tight.'

Leonora felt her face flush. She thought about her mum and dad being flaunted before the world, and Uncle Luther telling more whopping great lies about them. Anger coursed through her veins. 'Come on then,' she said, scooping

Twitchy up into her arms. 'Let's get back to SIG!'

'Very good,' said Brenda. 'We'll take the Rolls-Royce. And this time, young Jack, I think I'll drive.'

5
Card Games

It was getting very late as Leonora and the gang were driven by Brenda at breakneck (breakarm and breakleg) speed to the magnificent underground world of SIG. The headquarters were hidden deep below the ancient streets of

Mavenbridge. And now they were sitting in a high-tech room surrounded by computers, robots and stacks of the rogue Christmas cards.

'Maybe it's something to do with the gold star on the front?' suggested Jack, holding a card at arm's length and squinting at the design.

'Or an anagram of "On Your Marks"?' said Mildred, frowning. '*Smunky roaro? Sorry manouk?*'

Twitchy squarked from a nearby lab stool where he was bashing a card with one of his pebbles.

'Och, let's hear that music again,' said Captain Spang. He gently took the card from Leonora and opened it. Music shrieked around the sterile room, making them all wince.

'I'm not sure what I'm missing,' said Leonora. 'It's printed on A5, standard card. Inside is a mini speaker. There are no other markings.' She frowned and glanced anxiously at her watch. She

44

was jotting down a series of notes as Professor Puri, newly appointed SIG fellow, entered the lab.

'Prisha, happy holidays!' cried Mildred, rushing to hug her old friend and colleague.

Professor Puri greeted them each in turn. She then gestured to the card. 'I'm afraid this has our team stumped and so, with the deadline so tight, they've been thinking *laterally*.'

'Litterly? Lotterly?' Jack mashed the word.

Professor Puri smiled. 'No, *laterally* – it means thinking about a problem from a different angle.' She walked to the far end of the laboratory and flicked a switch. In an adjoining room, scientists in protective suits were conducting experiments. One had a card clamped in a vice and was hosing it down with what looked like liquid marmalade. Another was flame-grilling a card on a barbecue. A third had given a card to a dog to cover in slobber.

'Yeah, that's definitely looking at things . . . *differently*,' said Jack, staring wide-eyed at the scientists. 'Leo, what do *you* reckon?'

Leonora didn't reply. She'd taken her card to pieces and was examining each part of the speaker in turn with tweezers and a magnifying glass, searching for any clues. 'There's nothing strange about the electronics,' she muttered, taking off her glasses and rubbing her forehead with her wrist.

'No, our team couldn't find anything unusual either,' agreed Professor Puri. 'One of these cards has been sent to every household, which means it has the most brilliant brains in the world working on it. We're in a race against time to find the answer before they do.'

Leonora checked her watch. They had half an hour left. *Concentrate, Leo!* She assembled all the evidence. The three Gs for 'Great Gadget Games', the gold star, the **DING-DONG** music. None of it was making any sense. But then an idea sparked in her mind, like flint on steel. She took the card and placed it on a lightbox. Sure enough, she could see a secret message that read:

Gah, it's just another of Uncle Luther's totally unfunny jokes,' said Leonora, groaning. There were now only ten minutes to go. She took another deep breath. *I've got to solve this – it's on the tip of my brain!*

'Och, do you think we're looking in the wrong place?' asked Captain Spang. He passed Leonora the card's envelope. She took it and examined it carefully. Then, using a scalpel, she removed the stamp and placed it under a powerful microscope. Beneath the sticky glue she could just see a number 6.

'Captain, you're brilliant – I think we've got it!' she cried. 'Six on the stamp, one star, three Gs and two for **DING-DONG**. Six-one-three-two – try that number!'

'How do you know it's in that order?' asked Jack, worried.

'That's the logical order in which the items are revealed. Stamp first and then the star, the three Gs below it, and finally the **DING-DONG**.' *It has to be right.*

Professor Puri nodded, hurrying over to a computer. She loaded the Great Gadget Games website with only two minutes left. 'We'll need to enter you under a fake name,' she said.

'How's about "Lenny Cornflake"?' offered Mildred.

'O-K,' replied Leonora. 'Really sensible.'

Professor Puri tapped in L-E-N-N-Y C-O-R-N-F-L-A-K-E and the four-digit code. For one heart-stopping moment the screen went completely black. But then a dot appeared, getting larger and larger until Uncle Luther's grinning face filled the screen.

**Congratulations,
Lenny Cornflake,
you have successfully
entered the games!
Proceed to the next level.
Mavenbridge Millennium Stadium,
26 December, 6 a.m.**

'Yes!' cried Leonora, punching the air.

'Urgh!' said Jack. 'Trust your uncle to make it so early.'

'Yeah, that's when he used to wake me up to start inventing,' said Leonora, shuddering at the memory of all those pre-dawn starts. Twitchy bristled in agreement.

'Well, that doesn't give us much time,' said Brenda Spaniel, who'd stepped into the laboratory, clipboard in hand. 'We'll need to work through the night to perfect your disguises. Now, quickly, you must all come with me at once.'

6
Identigo

'You're not really going to dress me as a pot plant . . . are you?' asked Leonora, feeling a fizz of nervous excitement as they trotted behind Brenda down the winding corridors of Zone 4.

'Not unless things have gone very wrong,' Brenda replied, stopping in front of a shiny white door and clicking her fingers. It slid open to reveal a circular room that looked very much like an explosion in a fancy-dress shop. From floor to ceiling there were rails stuffed with every type of outfit: police uniforms and superhero capes, towering powdered wigs and fairy wings, skeleton jumpsuits and pirate swords.

'Och, it's a treasure trove!' exclaimed Captain Spang, gazing about. 'It reminds me of ma stage days,' he added, pulling out a taffeta ballgown.

'Welcome to our costume department,' said Brenda, 'although these aren't your average disguises.' She walked over to a steel box in the very centre of the room. It was bolted to the floor and covered in chains and padlocks.

'What's in there?' asked Jack. 'The Crown Jewels?'

'Something much more valuable,' replied Brenda, unlocking the box and removing a small rectangular object from inside. It had a flat screen, rainbow lights and a belt loop. She gestured for Leonora to raise her arms, and slipped the device round her waist. 'This gadget is called an **Identigo**,' explained Brenda. 'By studying plants and animals that can change their appearance –'

'Like chameleons and cuttlefish?' interrupted Jack.

'Exactly,' replied Brenda, 'and by mixing that knowledge with a dash of quantum physics we've created this temporary disguise device, just like the one I used to become your Christmas tree. Although this machine is far more powerful and less noisy. Let me demonstrate.'

Mildred, Captain Spang, Jack and Twitchy looked on as Brenda adjusted dials on the front of the box. She then stood back. Leonora waited for explosions or collywobbles or something but only felt a light breeze floof her face. Everyone else, however, looked properly freaked out.

'Ho, ho, ho!' cried Jack.

'Och, it's uncanny,' said Captain Spang, frowning.

'Is that really you, me little sugarplum?' asked Mildred.

Leonora turned towards Twitchy. He gave an

unconcerned squark, able to recognize her no matter her disguise. But when Brenda rolled out a floor-length mirror, Leonora gasped. She'd been transformed into an old man, complete with flowing white locks, red suit and generous belly.

'So, this is our festive setting. But we won't have you entering the games dressed like Santa,' said Brenda, tinkering with the rainbow buttons. Leonora watched in the mirror as she morphed again into a totally different nine-year-old kid with shorter hair and a jumper adorned with an L.

'That's just so . . . *strange*,' said Jack.

Leonora brushed trembling fingertips over her face and body. Everything felt normal. But her appearance had completely changed. She moved closer to the mirror to take a good look at herself. The only

hint that something was wrong was a pale bluish tinge at the very outer edges of her face. It was hardly noticeable except up very close. *Uncle Luther won't have a clue who I am.* 'It's . . . amazing!' she said, beaming at Brenda.

'Yes it is, although the technology is still unstable,' said Brenda with a tone of caution. 'We'll need your help to make a few improvements.'

'No problem,' she replied.

'And it also doesn't alter your voice, so you might need to change that too,' said Brenda, pressing buttons to reverse the disguise.

'OK, can do,' Leonora replied, sounding like a chipmunk with tonsillitis.

'That was so rubbish,' said Jack, snickering. Leonora elbowed him.

At that moment Professor Insignia, the head of SIG, entered the room. 'Good evening, everyone,' he said, giving them a formal nod.

'Excellent work on successfully cracking the code. And I can see that Professor Spaniel has been equipping you with your disguise.'

'We're nearing completion, sir,' said Brenda.

'Splendid. The sooner these games are over, the better. It seems the whole world's gone inventing-crazy.'

'What do you mean?' asked Leonora.

'I'm getting reports that a team from Germany has created webbed trainers for ducks.

The Canadian Children's Space Centre has just unveiled a satellite made of jam. And a nursery school in Cornwall is claiming to have invented raisins and the colour purple. It's all getting rather silly.'

Leonora grinned at Jack, who was trying to swallow his giggles.

'Although I do have some sensible news,' he added. 'We've got a new lead on HMS *Invisible*.'

Leonora felt her pulse quicken. 'Where is it?'

'There's a weak signal coming from the Cape of Good Grief. We need an expert navigator to help with the search. But without one of those, perhaps . . .' Professor Insignia let the words hang in the air, before looking over to Captain Spang.

'Och, you want me to find the boat?' The Captain gave a wide grin and adjusted his silk necktie. 'It would be ma honour, sir.'

'To reach that part of the ocean, you need to sail through the Slippery Straits and past the twin whirlpools of Kraken Cove,' said Brenda. 'It's a very dangerous route.'

'Aye, no bother,' said Captain Spang. 'Pretty sure I took a swan pedalo out there in 1989.'

'I don't likes the sounds of this, Angus,' said Mildred.

'Och, I'll be back before you know it,' he whispered, grasping her hand.

'Very well. It's decided,' said Professor Insignia. 'Leonora – or Lenny – will attend the games, and Captain Spang will set sail at first light.'

'I'm not staying here like a spare part waiting for news!' said Mildred.

'Professor Dribble,' said Brenda, 'I'll disguise you, Jack and Twitchy so that you can go to the games as Leonora's back-up. But you must stay undercover.'

'Oh, you know me, I'll keeps a low profile,' said Mildred, 'but if *that man* so much as lays a finger on her, I'll –'

'Thanks, Millie,' interrupted Leonora. 'I'll be fine. But, Captain, promise us – promise *me* – you'll come back safely?' She felt her throat get scratchy.

'Aye, of course, lassie. I'll be back in three shakes of a badger's bottom.'

Leonora frowned. 'OK . . . but, to be sure, let's use this.' She pulled out the **Bad Uncle Monitor** from her tool belt and tapped in commands to reprogram it. She then tucked a microchip inside Captain Spang's waistcoat pocket. 'There! I've tagged you,' she said, handing the updated BUM device to Mildred. 'This is now a **Captain Spang Monitor**. You'll be able to track his journey.'

'Och, I'm glad someone will,' said Captain Spang, giving her a wink.

'Perfect,' agreed Mildred. 'I'll keep my eyes on him.'

Leonora smiled and she, Mildred, Captain

Spang, Jack and Twitchy all came together in the centre of the room for a group hug. Leonora closed her eyes, trying to rekindle the festive warmth she'd felt earlier. But it was gone – replaced with cold reality. She had so many hurdles to jump before she got to the final. And if she made it, would her mum and dad really be there? Or would it be another of Uncle Luther's vile tricks? 'OK . . . let's do this,' she said, shaking away her doubts.

As they parted, Leonora put her hand into the centre of the circle, and everyone put theirs on top, with Twitchy's teeny paw last. They then threw them up in the air like superheroes, shouting, 'Let the games commence!'

7
Get Set

Leonora was definitely not feeling like a superhero a few hours later. She was standing outside Mavenbridge Stadium in the darkness before dawn. Cold wind nipped her cheeks. The sky looked like it was armed with water bombs. But, most worrying of all, the **Identigo** was behaving like a two-year-old: having a tantrum and throwing a wobbler at the same time.

'Leo, you need to reset it, sharpish,' whispered Jack.

'Huh, how come?'

'Because things have *gone very wrong* already. You can't enter the games disguised as *salad*!'

'What are you on about?'

Jack scrunched up his face and motioned towards her legs. Leonora pulled out a compact mirror from her tool belt. She gazed in amazement at her own bizarre reflection, half Lenny, half lettuce leaves.

'Yeah, OK, you're right,' she agreed, twiddling the knobs and trying to adjust the force field that she and Brenda had spent all night working on.

'Still no,' said Jack, as Leonora's upper body transformed into a tin of spaghetti hoops and her lower half became a leopard.

'I'm trying my best,' she hissed.

By now, hundreds of hopeful contestants and spectators were starting to gather at the stadium entrance. Despite the incredibly tight entry deadline, Leonora realized that beloved celebrity Uncle Luther could still pull in the crowds.

There was a **FWOOSH** sound as the stadium floodlights turned on, bathing them in dazzling fluorescent light.

'Quickly, Leo!' urged Jack, shielding her from view as the crowds swelled.

Leonora took a deep breath. She tapped numbers into the control panel and turned the settings from 'mild fakery' to 'full-body camouflage'. At last her appearance seemed to correct itself.

'That's better,' said Jack, looking relieved. He glanced over his shoulder. 'I reckon it's time to go inside.'

'Yes, but you'll needs to be careful,' whispered Mildred, arriving behind them, panting heavily.

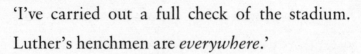

'I've carried out a full check of the stadium. Luther's henchmen are *everywhere*.'

Mildred was dressed in black bomber jacket, combat trousers and baseball hat, looking like a supermarket security guard. Twitchy, meanwhile, was on a lead beside her, brimming with annoyance. He was not happy about wearing false guard-dog ears, a set of dog booties and a bone-shaped collar with 'Fido' written on it.

Leonora stifled a giggle. 'Twitch, you look like such a good doggo,' she said in a cutesy voice, bending down to stroke him. He replied with a cross squark.

'But, young Jack, where's *your* disguise?' said Mildred. 'We can't risk you being spotted either.'

'Aha! Don't you remember what Luther said about me being "a nobody"?' he replied. 'It means I can totally blend in with the crowd. Check this out.' He slipped on a hoodie and hunched his shoulders. Leonora had to hand it to him – he looked instantly forgettable.

TOOOTY-TOOOT TOOOTY-TOOOOOOOOT!

Trumpets plarped in the damp morning air. Towering red doors at the stadium entrance swung open. There were whistles and cheers as the crowds surged forward.

'It's now or nevers, sweetheart,' said Mildred. 'Me, Jack and Twitchy will be watching you. You can do this!'

Leonora fought to ignore the fear bubbling up inside her. Jack gave her an encouraging dead arm. Twitchy barked. Mildred hugged her. She nodded and turned away, hurrying to join the tide of people surging through the gates.

Inside the stadium it felt like a carnival. A crowd of young brainiacs gathered on a large stage in the centre. The stands filled up with their supporters, singing and waving national flags.

Gazing around her, Leonora realized that, apart from her brief time at Snorebury Primary School (before she'd caused an emergency evacuation and hadn't returned), she'd never seen so many kids before. And they were all mini inventors, just like her! She felt a buzz of excitement and curiosity.

'Name?' asked a grouchy attendant, blocking her way.

'Erm . . . Lenny . . . Lenny Cornflake,' Leonora squeaked. She gave a nervous smile as the attendant scoured her list.

'Ah yes. Congratulations on getting this far. Head over there.' She waved over her shoulder without giving Leonora a second glance.

Leonora heaved a sigh of relief.

'This way please,' said another attendant, guiding Leonora on to the stage. Around a hundred tables were laid out in identical rows. Each was covered in tools and workshop equipment. Standing before her table, Leonora shielded her eyes from the bright lights. She willed the Identigo not to accidentally turn her into a family pack of Cheesy Tweetles or worse.

'Could I have your attention?' came Barry Tremendous's excitable voice. 'Take your seats – the games are about to begin!'

A hush settled on the audience. The lights went down. Smoke **FLOOOSHED** across the stage. Dozens of enormous screens hanging around the stadium suddenly lit up with a twirling pale blue heart. Leonora gasped – it was the secret logo of Uncle Luther's evil Iceheart operations.

'Welcome to the Great Gadget Games!' came another voice that Leonora knew only too well. She looked upwards. A hundred-foot image of Uncle Luther had appeared in the sky above their heads. He stared down at them all. Even though it was just a clever projection, Leonora could feel herself wilting beneath his gaze.

'Thank you all for coming,' said the Uncle Luther hologram. 'Contestants, you have two hours to construct the most impressive gadget from the equipment in front of you. I want the best invention since sliced bread. Now . . .

on your marks . . .

get set . . .

GO!'

Chapter 7 *and a Smidge*

The Ten Best Inventions Before/Since Sliced Bread

We're pausing this story to bring you a list of the human race's most brilliant brainwaves.

1   **The wheel**: it turns out the round shape is much better than earlier square and triangular designs.

2   **The nail**: really handy for holding stuff together like houses and boats. Less brilliant when stepped on in your bare tootsies.

3   **The compass**: invented
    by the Chinese and feared
    by geography students
    the world over.

4   **The printing press**:
    essential for creating hilarious and
    amazing books, like this one!

5   **The internal combustion
    engine**: although 'internal
    combustion' sounds like your
    teacher having a temper tantrum, this
    is actually the engine design that led
    to cars, planes and loads of other
    superfast vehicles.

6   **The telephone**: started off as
    two cans attached to a bit of string.
    Eventually evolved into smartphones
    (which have apparently become a bit
    popular?).

7   **The light bulb**: lighting up our lives and confusing the heck out of moths since the late nineteeth century.

8   **The internet**: a global computer network and humankind's most powerful communications tool. Mostly used for gawping at videos of hilarious pets.

9   **Penicillin**: who knew that mouldy stuff could fight bacterial infections? Well, nobody at first – it was discovered by accident – but later on it became a medical marvel. (For mould, fungus and surprise mushrooms, see also: Mildred's food.)

10 **Jelly Babies**: the pinnacle of all human foodie achievement. A sublime sweetie. Bite their silly little heads off.

8

We Love You, Luther

The stadium lights flashed back on. Leonora felt her thoughts (and knees) shaking like maracas. She looked down at the table of materials before her. Two hours? To make the best invention ever? In front of all these people? Her eyes darted about at the other contestants, who were already grabbing tools and setting to work. Above the noise she heard her parents' words of encouragement inside her head: *Never give up, Leonora!*

She searched the stands, imagining that they were watching her right at this very moment, cheering her on. What invention would make her stand out from the crowd? She realized that she knew better than anyone the kind of gadget that would catch Uncle Luther's eye. An idea flexed its biceps inside her brain, and she got going.

Leonora measured lengths of carbon fibre and cut out propellers, attaching them to little motors. She then built a speed controller and motion sensors. Before long she was completely absorbed in her project.

'Hey, that looks cool,' came a voice beside her, making her jump. A boy at the next table over was pointing at her machine.

'Huh? Oh, thanks,' she replied suspiciously.

'I'm Jian,' whispered the boy, 'and I'm really nervous. My hands are so shaky I can't fix this lever.'

'I've got butterflies too,' admitted Leonora. 'Do you want to borrow my glue gun?'

'Oh wow, that's really kind,' said Jian as he took the tool from Leonora. His grateful grin made her feel a happy buzz of friendship. 'Good luck,' he whispered.

As Leonora got back to work, a clock high above their heads ticked down the seconds of the challenge. Her hands were a blur of activity as she carefully drilled holes, soldered circuit boards and tested the joystick.

'That's it – time's up!' came host Barry Tremendous's voice. 'Step away from your tables!'

Already? Two hours had flown by in what had felt like two seconds. Leonora stood back, rubbing her forehead with her wrist.

'Well now, wasn't that nail-biting?' Barry said, over the loudspeaker, his face super-shiny on the big screens. 'And now it's time for Lord Luther to select the thirty best contestants. Prepare to be judged!'

The audience whistled and clapped as, to Leonora's horror, the real Uncle Luther took to the stage. Instead of his usual expensive clothes, he was wearing a slightly stained suit and an unsettling look that she didn't recognize. There were chants of 'Brightspark, Brightspark, Brightspark!' from the audience, who were delighted to see their inventing hero in real life.

Leonora felt the anger flooding inside her

about to burst its banks. Why couldn't these people see what he was really like? He was nothing but a liar and a cheat who couldn't even make his own inventions! And he was a parent-kidnapper too. Where *were* her mum and dad? She clenched her fists as Uncle Luther started to weave his way through the tables, pausing to inspect each gadget in turn.

'Now, how does this work?' he asked a little girl who had the flag of Uruguay pinned to her tracksuit. The girl blinked rapidly. She wound up her device – a cartwheeling robot cougar that squeaked her national anthem (one of the longest in the world). Uncle Luther looked bored only one verse in but slapped a rosette on it anyway.

'Congratulations. This is just the kind of gadget that I'm looking for at Brightspark Industries. You've made it through.' His voice was flat and held no emotion, but there were claps and cheers from the crowds.

Uncle Luther continued to stalk the stage, getting ever closer to Leonora. At last he stopped at Jian's table. With trembling fingers Jian managed to push his pipe-shaped device forward and pull its lever. A giant piece of toffee popcorn shot into the air above his table, before bursting into thousands of tiny bits. They rained down like an explosion at the cinema.

'Good work,' said Uncle Luther indifferently. He passed Jian a blue heart rosette. 'You're through to the next round.'

Leonora gave Jian a covert thumbs-up. But then Uncle Luther turned round and stepped towards her table, his terrible breath arriving a couple of seconds before he did. As he stood before her, she stifled the urge to gag.

'And who do we have here?' asked Uncle Luther, glaring down at her. 'Let's see what you've created.'

Leonora tried to meet his gaze. Half of her

wanted to sprint for the exit. The other half wanted to launch herself at him. Instead, she stood aside so he could see her gadget.

A miniature model of Uncle Luther was sitting on top of a drone. Leonora moved its joystick and the device launched upwards, hovering above the table and singing 'We love you, Luther! We love you, Luther! We love you, Luther!' in a tinny voice. Leonora then sent it to fly off around the stadium. The crowds went wild.

'An excellent invention!' he cried, as they watched the drone perform a victory lap. It was the first time he'd seemed even the slightest bit interested in the event. He handed Leonora a gold rosette. 'You're my star candidate. I'll be watching you very closely –' he read her name badge – 'Lenny Cornflake.' With that, he strode off to the next table.

Leonora let out the breath she'd been holding. Did he suspect her? She took out the pocket mirror and stole a quick look at her reflection. Her disguise still looked perfect. But the drone had been too clever, and now her uncle was watching her. She'd *have* to be more careful.

'Well done, everyone!' said Barry Tremendous on screen, after Luther had inspected the last few machines. 'What a fabulous festival of innovation. Rosette winners, please gather outside to be taken to your next challenge. And good luck . . . you'll need it.'

Just then, the monitors flicked off and a hissing sound came from the side of the stage. Blue and red smoke billowed out of machines all around them, making it impossible to see. Leonora coughed and spluttered. She counted one . . . two . . . ten seconds before the air had finally cleared.

She looked around, but Uncle Luther had vanished.

9
Get Ready

'Leo, you were amazing!' said Jack, as they were reunited outside the arena a little while later.

'Thanks . . .' she said, staring at his giant foam finger and even bigger bucket of Brightspark pick 'n' mix.

'I thoughts you were as cool as a cucumber,' agreed Mildred, arriving beside them, 'even with *that man* up close.' Twitchy squark-barked, hopping up at Leonora's legs and wagging his fake doggy tail.

'For a minute I was scared I'd given the game away,' she said. 'And I've no idea what's coming next.' Leonora glanced over at the gaggle of winners gathering by the entrance. *Star candidate.* She shivered. Cold drizzle flapped in her face, as if echoing her mood.

'Well, if I knows your uncle, there's sure to be a nasty twist,' said Mildred. 'We'll need some time to get you properly ready.'

'Yeah, maybe we can dash back to SIG and examine this,' agreed Leonora, pulling out the rumpled rosette. 'It could hold clues to the next round.'

'Erm, I don't think you'll have time for that,' said Jack, as a large coach with blacked-out windows rolled down the street. It stopped beside the stadium entrance, brakes shushing. The door opened and a team of stern-looking staff wearing red jumpsuits and headsets marched out. They approached the winners and started ushering them aboard.

'B-but I can't do the next challenge straight away!' whispered Leonora, feeling as if someone had just tipped cold dishwater down her neck. 'I – I need to recharge the batteries on the Identigo. What if they run out?'

'I dunno,' said Jack, 'but I think we've been spotted. Split up!' He turned on his heels and hurried away down the street, pulling Twitchy on a lead behind him. Mildred gave Leonora a quick squeeze before hurrying away too, in the opposite direction. One of the women from the coach was striding over.

'Lenny Cornflake?' she said, gesturing towards her name badge.

'Um . . . yes?' Leonora just about managed to squeak out the word.

'Congratulations on reaching the next round of the games. You must come with me right away.'

Leonora's heart thudded against her ribs as she followed the woman to the coach.

'Come along, we don't have all day!' shouted another usher, as Leonora reluctantly clambered aboard. All the other contestants seemed to be making new friends, laughing and joking. Leonora couldn't see Jian anywhere, so she slumped down in a seat by herself, choking back tears and annoyance. Jack had just walked off and left her in her hour of need. What sort of friend was he? What if her disguise failed? At best she wouldn't be able to complete the next round, and at worst . . . She shuddered. *It's fine. I can win this without him*, she thought, folding her arms.

'Now then, make yourselves comfortable,' said the driver into a microphone. 'We've got a long journey ahead.' With that, the coach pulled away from the stadium.

Leonora leaned her cheek against the cool glass of the window, and gazed out. *I don't need Jack. I'm better off alone.* But a few moments later she realized that unfortunately she wasn't on her own after all.

'So, Lenny *Corn*flake,' came a sneering voice from behind her. 'What sort of stupid name is that?'

Leonora turned round. 'Huh, what?'

'I said, whoever heard of someone called "Cornflake"? That's just, like, mega *embarrassing*.' A boy with smooth brown hair and a turned-up nose was leaning over the back of her seat and staring down at her.

Leonora glanced at his name badge: Bonald Snootle. 'I, erm . . . it's, um . . . none of your business,' Leonora stammered, feeling her face get hot.

'Saw your drone,' he carried on. 'Thought it was really lame. Don't think you'll win the next round, *star candidate*. You're nowhere near as smart as me.'

Leonora opened her mouth to defend herself but then shut it again, feeling the total injustice of being picked on by someone called Bonald (and feeling miffed with Mildred for picking an equally silly name for her). She hunched back down in her seat and tried to block out the giggles that were now rippling around the back of the coach.

They sped on through the grey streets and past the outskirts of town. Houses soon gave way to rolling hills and fields. Leonora checked her watch and tried to work out their speed and in which direction they were heading. But the scenery all looked the same.

'Please, miss,' said one of the younger children, 'are we nearly there yet?'

'Candidates are not allowed to ask questions,' an usher snapped. 'You're being taken to a *secret* location, not a holiday camp. We won't arrive until the morning.'

'I heard the next challenge is out on the moors,' whispered Bonald. 'The countryside around here is totally haunted. Full of ghouls and ghosts.'

'Yeah,' said a teenage girl across the aisle, 'and the locals all have, like, zombie heads and webbed teeth!' All the older children at the back of the coach laughed.

Leonora shivered. Ghosts? Zombies? *There's no such thing*, she thought, trying to use her common sense to wrestle away scaredy-cat fears.

As they drove on, an uneasy quiet fell inside the coach, broken only by sniffs from some of the younger children. Leonora's imagination had started to run wild. Whatever Uncle Luther had in store for them, she knew one thing for certain: it was going to be much more dangerous than ghosts and zombies.

10
In the Pines

'Wakey-wakey, eggs and bakey!' called the coach driver.

Leonora awoke from a fretful sleep. She lifted her head and rubbed her cricked neck. It took a few seconds for her to remember where she was – remember *who* she was. She looked at the window and was relieved to see Lenny's reflection staring back, although a red warning light flashed on the **Identigo**. But then she suddenly remembered something – wasn't there a way to recharge batteries using the acid from everyday fruit?

Her hand shot up. 'Um, miss?' she asked one

of the nearby ushers. 'I don't suppose I could have some oranges for breakfast? Like, twenty of them?'

'We don't have time for that,' the woman snapped. 'Now, all of you, come along.'

One by one the candidates got to their feet and filed off the coach.

'See you later, *loser*,' Bonald sneered at Leonora as he pushed his way to the front. Ten brilliantly witty insults popped into her head, but only after he'd gone.

They'd travelled overnight and the coach had come to a stop inside an enormous pine forest. Trees towered overhead. Black branches brushed the pale morning sky. The air smelled of moss and mulch. The children followed red-suited grown-ups along a narrow path. After several minutes, they arrived at a clearing.

Leonora gasped. Before them was the most enormous junkyard she'd ever clapped eyes on.

Everywhere she looked were towering piles of scrap metal, discarded engines, tools, battered vehicles, spare tyres and old oil drums. It was a recycling paradise. Despite her nerves, she couldn't stop feeling a wave of excitement too. It *was* pretty much her idea of a holiday camp.

'Contestants, welcome to the Feargrim Forest!' came a cheerful voice.

Standing on a wooden-pallet platform in the centre of the clearing was Barry Tremendous. He was sporting a shiny suit and outrageous quiff (that was less of a hairdo, more of a hair-don't).

It took Leonora a few moments to realize that they were being filmed by hidden cameras in the trees. The thirty remaining candidates gathered before Barry. Leonora hung back, trying to work out an escape route in case she needed a sharp exit, but the forest looked thick.

'I'm here to reveal your second challenge,' said Barry, 'and it's an ingenious one!' He winked into a camera. Fake game-show laughter boomed from a speaker behind him. 'You need to build a vehicle using only the junk you see around you. Then we want you to drive it to a special meeting point by midnight. The first ten contestants to use their brainpower and find their way out of the forest will be put forward to the grand final!'

Several of the teenagers cheered and punched the air. The younger children swapped worried glances. Leonora felt her own tummy flip. Barry pulled on a rope that unfurled a map. It showed a location sixty kilometres to the north.

'You have 57,600 seconds, or 960 minutes, or sixteen hours to complete the task and meet us here.' He tapped the map with his finger. 'Best of luck, and your time starts – now!'

With that, an air horn sounded above their heads. For a couple of seconds no one moved a muscle, then all the children scattered like startled pigeons. They ran around the junkyard grabbing metal pipes, broken kettles, old kitchen sinks and all manner of other battered gear.

Leonora, meanwhile, was forced to slowly edge towards the trees. The **Identigo** was making a weird whining sound, like it would break at any moment. She watched helplessly as the other children got a head start and as Barry Tremendous and all the grown-ups made their way back to the coach.

'But you – you can't leave us here on our own,' said one of the smaller boys as the adults marched past, practically knocking him over.

Barry laughed cheerily. 'You didn't think a celeb like me would spend all day in this rubbish dump, did you?' With that, he strode off through the forest, leaving the children to fend for themselves.

Rain started to pitter-patter through the branches, then **SPLOSH** in big drops. Before long it was (to use the technical term) completely *razzing it down*. Some of the younger children began to cry, which made Leonora feel another wave of anger, like she was about to burst a valve or blow a gasket. Or both.

This was so *typical*. Trust Uncle Luther to leave thirty kids unattended in a spooky forest with mountains of lethal junk and only TV cameras for babysitters! It was just about the worst reality TV show ever. And, to add to her frustration, the Identigo was now going bananas. As she reached the shelter of the trees, it began cycling through random disguises – a

bunch of tulips, a loo brush, a mammoth. Any second now her cover would be blown!

'*Pssst*, Leo.'

Leonora spun round. Peeking out from a spindly tree trunk twenty feet away, inside the woods, she could just see a blonde tuft of hair. And, below it, a set of magnificent whiskers.

Her heart did a handspring. She checked that none of the other kids were watching, before sprinting over. 'Jack, Twitch – how on earth did *you* get here?'

'We snuck into the luggage hold beneath the coach. Worst night's sleep ever,' Jack groaned, rubbing his face.

'But I thought . . .'

'That we'd left you?' Jack rolled his eyes. Twitchy jumped up for a cuddle.

'Um, I wasn't sure *where* you'd gone,' she said, feeling a gigantic wave of gratitude and relief. 'I'm just . . . so glad you're here.'

'Mildred tried to squash in too, but then trusted us to come alone. She's back at SIG, leading a team tracking the Captain.'

'Definitely the best plan,' said Leonora. 'She'd be spotted straight away. Talking of which, I've got a major problem.'

Leonora set Twitchy back down and grabbed

103

the **Identigo**. The whining sound grew louder, the blue tinge around her appearance got brighter and – **SSSSIIIIIZZZZ** – Lenny turned back into Leonora.

'Urgh, I see what you mean. We can't have you looking like *that*,' said Jack with a cheeky grin. 'What can I do?'

'You can shush,' she said, smiling back, 'but then . . . can you find a car battery? That should fix it.' Jack nodded, pulled up his hoodie and walked away.

By now, the clearing was a frenzy of activity. Children were welding, sawing, hammering and drilling all over the place. There were shouts and occasional explosions, sparks flying. Five minutes later, Jack had returned, lugging what looked like a large lunch box.

'That's perfect!' whispered Leonora.

Jack gave a casual shrug, like it was nothing, which made Leonora's chest get tight. She realized that she couldn't do any of it without him – and that he'd never leave her. *Bestest best friend ever.*

'Can you quit gawking and help me?' he said.

'Oh yeah, sorry.' Leonora grabbed one side of the heavy battery and together they set it down beside a thick tree trunk. She slipped off the **Identigo** and rummaged in her tool belt for a length of electrical wire.

'Hurry,' urged Jack, keeping watch.

Leonora took a penknife and flicked off the Identigo's casing, then carefully attached a small clamp from the car battery to her power supply. To her relief the lights went orange – it was recharging!

'Once that's fixed, what machine are you gonna make?' whispered Jack. 'They've got a big lead on you,' he added, waving towards the other contestants.

'I dunno,' she whispered back, watching as

Bonald snatched a fuel can from Jian and shoved him out of the way. 'I just know that mine has to be better than *his*.'

Leonora watched a girl building a pair of steam-powered roller skates. Another boy was welding tank-style caterpillar tracks on to a tiny tricycle. It made her remember all the weird and wonderful vehicles she'd made or fixed: the *Aquabolt* submarine, the desert Dromad, her crisp-packet kayak.

'Come on, come on!' she muttered, crouching back down to check the Identigo's battery.

At long last the lights went green. 'That's it, I can start!' Leonora quickly slipped the belt back on, twiddled the dials and returned to her Lenny Cornflake disguise. She gave Twitchy and Jack a determined look, and turned and hurried away from the safety of the trees. But just as she was about to start work –

'Ah, there you are, Cornflake!' Bonald jumped down from the top of a nearby dumper truck, crowbar in hand. He gazed up at the cameras and lowered his voice. 'Did you get a bit lost? I bet you've been in the woods, crying for your mummy and daddy.'

Leonora flinched. 'Why don't you leave me alone!'

'I'm the real winner here, little star candidate –' he prodded her shoulder – 'and

I'm taking that top prize. Little swotty squirts like you aren't going to stop me!'

Leonora felt dizzy. She was so far behind the others and time was running out. But then a light bulb flickered inside her brain, as a brilliant thought occurred to her.

'Of course you're going to win,' she said, launching a timid smile in Bonald's direction. 'You're just *sooooo* much brainier than me that I bet you've already spotted those.' Leonora pointed behind him towards a stack of monster-truck tyres.

'Yeah, finders keepers,' he said with a smirk. 'Losers weepers.'

As Bonald jogged away, Leonora saw her chance to give him the slip. She hurried over to the opposite side of the clearing, ready to test whether her brilliant idea would work. Because if it didn't . . .

. . . she was in deep trouble.

11
Teamwork Makes the Dream Work

'Contestants, the time is ten a.m. You have just fourteen hours left to complete the challenge!'

The command boomed about the forest. Leonora spotted Jian and ran over. He was with a couple of the youngest girls. They were busy building vehicles that looked like a light sneeze could collapse them.

'Hey! How are you getting on?' asked Leonora as she approached.

Jian stopped hammering and looked up. 'Hello again, Lenny,' he said with a bright smile. 'Er, not brilliantly, to be honest.'

'Well, why don't we team up?' she said.

'There's no rule to say we can't work together to make something really awesome!'

There was an awkward pause. Then to Leonora's relief, Jian and the other kids nodded. Her light bulb of optimism burned brighter. *If you can't beat 'em, join 'em.* Uncle Luther wouldn't be expecting them to help each other. He'd assume that all the contestants were like him – selfish, only out for number one.

'I'm Scarlett,' said a girl with long plaits.

'And I'm Meera,' said the other girl, giving a shy grin.

Leonora smiled back, pulling a notebook from her pocket. 'I'm Lenny. And I bet together we'll come up with an amazing machine. No idea is too ridiculous!'

Leonora drew a quick sketch of a ninety-foot pogo stick and a hammock catapult, but scribbled them all out again. Maybe those were

a *bit* ridiculous. She screwed up her face and tapped the pencil on her chin.

'The woods are so thick that loads of engines won't be able to just drive through them,' said Meera, gesturing about.

'And we don't want to disturb the trees or wildlife,' agreed Jian.

Leonora swiftly drew another diagram on a fresh page. She ripped it out and pinned it to a nearby tree. 'So how about this instead?'

The kids all studied the design, then started adding their own ideas.

'I love building turbo engines,' said Jian, 'so I could do that.'

'And I can fix the bodywork,' offered Meera, drawing some cool aerodynamic fins.

'Leave the launch pad to me,' said Scarlett. 'What shall we call it?'

'It's – it's a **Treetop Travelator**,' replied Leonora. 'The first in the world!'

They all exchanged excited looks, which made Leonora feel a sudden burst of joy. On Crabby Island she'd only ever worked alone. She'd spent long hours up in her workshop, pausing only to eat mouldy sandwiches or be shouted at by Uncle Luther (often at the same time). But out here in this soggy forest she had a gang, a group, a tribe – other kids to share her passion for inventing, all united in a common purpose. It felt as if a symphony was playing all around them, swelling to a blissful crescendo!

'You know that's cheating.'

The music in Leonora's head screeched off. She turned round. *Bonald*.

'The rules didn't say anything about working alone or as a team,' she said.

'Yeah, well, I'd have thought that's obvious, Cornflake. You're all going to fail this challenge.'

Leonora stuck her chin out. 'We'll see about that. And we have to work together; it's not safe to leave young kids out here in the forest past midnight.'

As soon as she said this, a ghostly **HOWLING** sound like wolves murdering oboes came echoing through the trees. Even Bonald looked unsure.

'Yeah, well, I'm not staying around here,' he said. 'See you losers later.'

Leonora watched him scurry off. 'Don't listen to bullies,' she said, picking up a wrench and gripping it. 'Rules are made to be . . . **STRETCHED**. Now let's get to the final!'

Over the next few hours Leonora and her gang worked together like happy honeybees. Leonora directed the search for cables, metal tubing, sockets, sprockets, springs and brackets.

Meera began welding old troughs together to form the frame. Jian cleaned spark plugs and fixed the engine. And eventually the Travelator started to look like a real vehicle. It had smooth sides, a pointy nose cone and a low windscreen. Underneath were several small tyres with grippy rubber knobbles.

'Right then, we're going to need a very big run-up,' said Leonora, wiping her filthy hands on her tracksuit, 'otherwise it might get a bit . . . *splintery.*'

By now, it was late evening. A pale moon ghosted the sky. It sounded as if the wolves had swapped to trombones, as their menacing howls grew lounder.

'Quickly, everyone, climb aboard,' urged Leonora.

All around them the older kids revved their engines and drove away, the lights of their contraptions fading into the forest. Leonora tried hard to ignore them and concentrate on her own plan. But what if the Travelator didn't work? What if she couldn't reach the final? What if she lost her parents again? She clenched her jaw. *I've beaten him three times already – there's no way I'm going to lose now!*

'Right, time to hit the tree – I, erm, mean, the road,' she said, hopping into the driver's seat and turning the ignition. The engine gave a throaty ROAR. A ghastly niff like mouldy cheese mixed with hot tarmac filled the air. Green and blue sparks flew from the rear.

'Don't forget *us*,' cried Jack, as he bounded from the trees clutching Twitchy.

'As if I ever would,' she whispered, watching

Jack land face-down, legs akimbo, in the seat behind her.

'These are our co-pilots,' Leonora explained, shooting a nervous glance at Jian and the gang. 'Er, late entrants to the competition.'

The other kids looked too scared to worry about stowaways. They were sitting in pairs, their eyes as big as hula hoops.

Jack and Twitchy squiggled upright. Leonora threw a jumper over their heads to hide them from the TV cameras.

'Please tell me you're not planning to drive this thing at that massive tree,' Jack said, peeking out.

'OK, I won't tell you. It'll be a fun surprise.'

Jack groaned. 'What speed?'

'Over sixty miles per hour.'

'And then what?'

'Leave those little details to me,' she said, flicking various switches on the dashboard.

Leonora stared at the skate ramp that Scarlett had constructed against the tallest pine, a hundred metres away. It was lit up on either side by rows of recycled fairy lights like a runway. She felt her stomach fold itself into more knots than an octopus doing origami. It was now or never. Sink or swim. Kill or cure. (Hopefully not that last one.) They had less than two hours to get to the meeting point!

'Passengers, this is your pilot speaking,' she said, hoping her tone sounded bright rather than bum-clenchingly terrified. 'Please ensure that your chairs are in an upright position, tray tables are stashed and seat belts are on. We'll be cruising at a height of one hundred feet. And . . . erm . . . there might be some turbulence!'

12
Perfect Dismount

Sometimes in life it's good to see what's coming. To have a clear view of the road up ahead and all the obstacles in your way.

Leonora decided that this was most definitely NOT one of those times, as the Travelator dashed at top speed towards their patchy ramp.

BRRRRRRUMMMMM!

She clamped her eyes shut, grabbed Twitchy's teeny soft paw in her damp palm, slammed her foot on the accelerator and –

EEEEEEEEEAAAARRRRKK!!!

Everyone screamed as the machine hit the slope. But instead of a splintered catastrophe, Leonora was relieved to feel the Travelator tip ninety degrees and judder its way up the tree. Up they climbed like a racing caterpillar, knobbly tyres gripping the bark. In just a few moments they'd reached the top of the leafy canopy and then –

'Hold on!' she cried, as the Travelator tipped forward to become level again. Leonora pulled

a lever at her feet and the tyres tucked into little compartments underneath the vehicle, leaving a smooth surface for the machine to glide across the treetops.

'We did it!' cried Leonora, jabbing the air with her fist.

'**WAHEY!!**' chorused the children, high-fiving and hugging each other.

'Is it over yet?' muttered Jack, his head firmly tucked between his knees.

'**SQUOOKY-SQUOOK?**' groaned Twitchy.

'Ha, you cowardy custards! Look – you're missing the view!' Leonora gazed out across the forest, feeling like a golden eagle in flight. A dark carpet of mighty trees stretched beneath them as far as the eye could see. Glittery stars filled the sky above their heads.

'OK, I'm impressed, Leo . . . nny,' said Jack, finally sitting up and surveying the scene. Twitchy let out a reluctant woof of approval too. Leonora was pleased that, just as they'd planned, the Travelator was leaving the woods and wildlife below totally undisturbed, gently surfing over the topmost branches.

'Lenny, you need to turn thirty degrees to your left,' said Scarlett, who was examining a map and compass. 'Keep steady – that's good.'

After a few more minutes, Leonora checked her watch. It was now 11.30 p.m. They had half an hour to reach the checkpoint and they were making good time, but then –

'Lenny!' called Jian. 'How are we gonna get down again?'

Leonora felt a nasty tang fill her mouth. She realized that she'd been so focused on getting them up and out of the forest, she hadn't given any thought to their landing! 'Yes! Erm . . . should we have a little meeting about that?' she shouted over her shoulder. 'Best idea wins . . . um . . . loads of Jelly Babies!'

'Leo,' Jack muttered, 'seriously?'

'Yeah, well, I've had one or two other things on,' she mumbled back, feeling dread welling up inside her.

'The checkpoint's now ten kilometres away,' shouted Scarlett.

'How about we jump out at the exact moment of impact?' said Meera.

'Or use a big parachute?' offered Jian.

'Gah, didn't pack one,' said Leonora. 'Come on, you lot, we're the brainiest kids on the planet! Surely we can think up a landing plan in the next, erm, ten minutes!'

'Eight minutes and twenty-four seconds,' corrected Scarlett.

Up ahead, Leonora could now see the forest's edge coming into view. And just beyond that was a beacon with the three Gs of the 'Great Gadget Games' shining out of it. If she slowed down, they'd lose momentum and plummet through the canopy. There *had* to be another solution. *Think, think!*

'We need, like, a stretchy rubber rope or something,' she said, 'to hook over the final tree and stop us falling.'

'Great, does anyone just happen to have some

elastic handy?' cried Jack. 'Knickers, underpants – something on a really massive scale?'

The kids all shook their heads, but then Jian piped up.

'What about using our scarves?'

'Perfect!' shouted Leonora, trying to hide the note of panic in her voice.

'Five minutes, eleven seconds!' cried Scarlett, as the kids started knotting their knitwear together. They created a big loop at one end and secured the other to the back seats.

'Two minutes, fifty-three seconds!'

Leonora could now see the field they needed to land in approaching fast. She felt her pulse pounding in her ears. 'Everyone, hold tight and prepare for my signal!' she cried.

Ten metres.

'Nearly there!'

Five metres.

'Wait for it!'

Two metres.

'Throw the rope!'

Leonora slammed on the brakes as they approached the final tree. The Travelator made a **SCROOOCHING** sound. There was an epic pause, as if the planets themselves had decided to stop spinning. Then the Travelator plunged its way down the tree trunk, as they all screamed. But Jian managed to lob the scarf-rope, looping it round the top of the tree.

The Travelator, five small children and one dog-otter hung five metres from the ground, swinging wildly from side to side. After several hair-raising (and pant-widdling) moments, the machine finally came to a stop. There was a huge collective sigh from behind her, but just as Leonora was about to announce that everything was fine, dandy and tickety-boo, the scarf-rope unravelled itself from the branch above and they fell downwards.

Fortunately some vegetables came to the rescue.

13
Checkpoint Checkmate

'Ooof, who left those here?' groaned Leonora from beneath a pile of parsnips.

'Wild guess – a farmer?' replied Jack, brushing broccoli from his hair.

The Travelator had landed upright and ploughed through a bed of winter crops before coming to a juddering halt. The kids all emerged from the machine and clambered out from underneath stacks of leafy greens one by one. Leonora breathed a huge sigh of relief to see that no one was hurt.

'That was amazing!' said Jian, giving her a fist bump.

'Yeah, your idea really worked,' agreed Scarlett.

Leonora felt her cheeks flush. 'It wasn't just me; we did it together . . . We're a *team*.'

'I hate to break up the party,' said Jack, grabbing Twitchy, 'but we'd better hide – and you'd better run!' He pointed to a platform a hundred metres away. It had a big golden button in the centre and banners of Uncle Luther on either side. Leonora wasn't sure which made her feel queasier – the Travelator crash or the pictures.

'Lenny, leg it!' called Jack, snapping her back into the moment.

Several other competitors were now emerging from the forest on their makeshift vehicles. Leonora turned and started sprinting as fast as her (incredibly wibbly-wobbly) legs could carry her.

'Come on – hurry!' she cried, encouraging

the other kids to run too. Scarlett, Jian and Meera reached the podium just ahead of her as a clock began chiming midnight. Leonora raced behind them, counting one, two . . . nine other kids that had made it. With her last ounce of strength, she reached the stage and leaped into the air. But just before she could push the golden button, Bonald appeared from the other side of the platform and thumped it first.

'HA!' he cried. 'I said I'd beat you, Cornflake.'

Leonora landed in a crumpled heap on stage but sprang back up and counted the kids around her. To her dismay she realized she'd failed; she wasn't in the top ten!

TOOOTY-TOOOT TOOOTY-TOOOOOOOT!

Annoying trumpet music blasted again. The field was suddenly floodlit. Golden streamers launched into the night sky. Ticker tape fluttered down. Barry Tremendous appeared on the scene with his camera crew. Leonora shuffled off stage as the winners stood in the limelight.

'Well, that was a cliffhanger,' Barry was saying, 'but congratulations to our fantastic finalists!'

Leonora felt her stomach churn. *I've blown it. I'll never save Mum and Dad!* She kicked the ground. Hot tears stung her cheeks.

'Tune in next time for the grand final of the Great Gadget Games!' said Barry, winking into the camera.

Then, almost as quickly as it had started, the TV circus ended. The music stopped. Equipment was switched off. Production crew herded exhausted and hungry children towards a waiting coach. Barry strode off without so much as a smile.

Leonora watched from the shadows, realizing that showbiz was every bit as hollow as she'd imagined. That's why Uncle Luther loved it so much.

The following morning, Leonora, Jack and a dog-eared Twitchy were safely back at SIG. They'd been picked up from the field by Brenda Spaniel, who had disguised herself as a local parsnip farmer and driven them back at record speed on a jet-propelled tractor. They were now being bombarded with breakfast buns and hot chocolate by a distraught-looking Mildred.

'We watched the whole thing,' she cried. 'I couldn't believe he'd make a kids' competition so bloomin' dangerous!'

'Yeah,' agreed Jack, 'as if reality TV isn't stupid enough.'

'Did my disguise hold up?' asked Leonora. 'I tried to avoid the cameras.'

'Perfectly,' said Professor Insignia. 'You looked like Lenny throughout the show. And you should be proud of yourself, Leonora. It's only thanks to your excellent teamwork that you and the younger children escaped the forest unhurt.'

Leonora cast her mind back to the previous night – hurtling over black treetops at over sixty miles an hour then landing in a pile of vegetables. She decided not to argue the point.

'But I didn't make the final,' she groaned, pushing her plate away. 'I've missed my chance to get inside the secret studio, to rescue Mum and Dad. And what about the Captain? Is there any news from him?'

Mildred took the **Captain Spang Monitor** from her pocket and showed Leonora. Red lines criss-crossed the screen like a toddler's colouring book. 'I think he's going the long way,' she said, 'but I bet he'll find that silly ship in no time!'

Leonora heard the forced cheerfulness in Mildred's voice. Her heart sank faster than one of the Captain's boats.

'All is not lost,' said Professor Puri, quietly entering the room and placing a laptop on the table before them. 'There's been a new development. It appears you'll get another chance to reach the final . . . although there's a big catch.' She hit return on the keyboard and a video began to play. Uncle Luther appeared on screen. He was standing on a large stage in front of a red velvet curtain.

'What an exciting contest we've seen so far,' he said, letting out a weird high-pitched laugh. 'The games have uncovered so much inventing talent. Here are our finalists.' The camera panned sideways to reveal the winners wearing gold sashes, with Bonald at the front.

'Now each great nation on earth has made some amazing advances,' Uncle Luther continued. 'For example, the Chinese gave us paper, the ancient Greeks created clockwork and the English pioneered . . . the sandwich.'

'*Amazing*,' muttered Jack.

'But good innovations are boring. To liven things up, I've decided to add a little twist to the Great Gadget Games. There's a new wild-card place up for grabs. But I don't want your best inventions . . . I want your *worst*.'

Leonora and Jack shared worried looks. Twitchy growled beneath the table.

'And when I say "worst", I mean I want the most deadly and downright dangerous creations that can be dreamed up,' said Uncle Luther with a feverish grin. 'Send them in before 29 December to win your wild-card place, and join us for the grand final here at my secret TV studio. The best of luck to you all!'

Chapter 13 *and 3 Ounces*

The WORST Inventions Before/Since Sliced Bread

Humans have come up with some very stupid ideas, from underpants for hands to inflatable dart boards, pocket chainsaws and spelling tests. Here are a few of our greatest brain-blurps:

In bronze medal position:
hydrogen blimps

Also called airships, these enormous flying machines were popular in the 1930s. Imagine a birthday balloon shaped like a rugby ball

but on a really **MAHOOSIVE** scale. Originally filled with cheap hydrogen gas to make them float, the problem was that they easily caught fire. After a few major disasters, scientists swapped to helium gas instead, which doesn't burn.

In silver medal position: dynamite

A Swedish chemist called Alfred Nobel dreamed up this idea (although not for use in Christmas crackers). He was trying to make it safer for workmen to handle explosives. Unfortunately, the military got hold of it and used dynamite for blowing up all sorts of stuff, causing widespread destruction. In fact, Nobel felt so guilty about his terrible creation, he started an annual award to celebrate good innovations called the Nobel Prize. The moral of the story: don't let anyone turn your good intentions into bad inventions.

In gold medal position:
grabby-claw machines

They might seem like innocent fairground attractions, but grown-ups will agree they're one of the world's most devastating ideas, designed to make small children very cross indeed. You can kiss your cash goodbye as the claw strokes the teddy bear, before dropping it again. A clear winner of the worst invention EVER.

Honourable mention:
the parachute suit

Is it a very floppy coat or is it a parachute? The answer is both and that's the problem. It was invented by a tailor called Franz Reichelt in 1912, and he was so convinced that he'd created a new type of perfect parachute for aviators that he jumped off the Eiffel Tower to prove it. This did not go very well. Life lesson: sometimes overconfidence can be your downfall.

14
The Blunder Bureau

'So *that's* a good-news-bad-news sandwich,' muttered Jack.

'Yeah,' agreed Leonora, frowning. 'I can only reach the final by creating a bad gadget that Uncle Luther will use for awful schemes, like mind control or something.'

'Like them kitten videos on the internet?' asked Mildred.

'Nothing could be that powerful,' whispered Jack.

'This is certainly a worrying twist,' agreed Professor Insignia, who was now circling the room, hands clasped behind his back. 'If I know Luther, he plans to steal ideas for deadly gadgets and get Brightspark Industries to manufacture them, causing global chaos. We simply can't allow the contest to go ahead.'

Leonora nodded. She had a flashback to BrightWorld and the words her uncle had whispered to her there –

If I can't be happy, no one can.

So this was his latest spiteful plan. He'd use the games to find and unleash bad technology on the world, then every country would have to pay him to reverse the effects. He'd make money from mayhem, moolah from misery. A man who couldn't experience joy himself would ensure that everyone else was unhappy too!

'Well, if it's *bad* inventions he's after,' said Professor Puri, 'I think it's high time Leonora was given access to Zone Thirteen.'

Professor Insignia paused, furrowed his brow.

'That's one of our most secret areas. It simply isn't safe for any of the projects in that zone to . . . escape.'

Escape? Leonora felt as if her curiosity had just strapped itself to a spaceship and launched into orbit.

Aside from their quick look inside the costume department, she'd only been allowed into super-boring Zone 1 of SIG, where scientists studied leaves or drying paint or whatever. And Professor Insignia had been very clear: *SIG is no place for children*. But was he about to change his mind? She arranged her face to look eager but trustworthy.

Professor Insignia was having none of it. 'It's too great a security risk,' he said firmly.

'Well, then Leonora won't be able to stop Luther,' said Mildred, annoyed. 'She needs a bad gadget to win her place at the games, and time is running out!'

'Pleeease,' pleaded Jack. 'We deffo won't tell anyone what's in there. Cross our hearts and hope to die.'

'Or ideally *not* die,' corrected Leonora. Twitchy stood on his hind legs and pressed his webby paws together, eyes wide.

Everyone was quiet for a few moments. Then Professor Insignia let out a sigh. 'Very well. I will allow you access. Choose the device in Zone Thirteen that you think will most appeal to your uncle.'

There was a *ping* noise. Professor Insignia checked his pager. 'Ah, Professor Dribble and I must return to my office – urgent report on HMS *Invisible*.'

'Wait! What's the latest?' asked Leonora.

'I can't tell you yet, Leonora. And I need you to focus on your current task. You'll have to travel to Zone Thirteen without me and you must be *incredibly* careful. I'm trusting you.'

'We won't let you down,' said Leonora, giving him a firm nod.

Several hours later, Leonora was having a strong word with herself about being a total nosy parker. Professor Insignia had escorted her, Jack and Twitchy back to SIG's main entrance, a vast stone chamber at the centre of the underground complex with fifteen gleaming white doors. After opening the door labelled ZONE 13, they'd been strapped into a shuttle car that was now whizzing them down a black tunnel at unbelievable speed.

Jack shuffled in his seat. 'How much longer, do you reckon?'

'Zone Thirteen is miles underground from SIG headquarters,' replied Leonora, 'to stop thieves getting in.'

'Or dangerous stuff getting out,' said Jack, his eyes like dinner plates.

Leonora could feel Twitchy's whiskers

quivering against her neck. She hugged him even tighter.

SWOOOORSH! The shuttle car came to a stop. Leonora, Jack and Twitchy climbed out. Before them was a black door with BLUNDER BUREAU written on it. Leonora pressed her fingers against a wall scanner, recited a medieval French poem and all twenty code words, just as Professor Insignia had told her to do. The door slid open.

Leonora blinked, adjusting her eyes to the gloom. They stepped into a long and dimly lit cavern. There was a stale whiff in the air. Enormous glass pods lined either side of the path. As they took timid steps forward, Leonora's pulse thrummed with fear.

'What is *that*?' she whispered.

To their right they could see a gigantic robotic hyena lounging inside a pod, tongue lolling. It unexpectedly leaped up and started pawing at

the glass with claws like kitchen knives, a dreadful metallic howling sound escaping its jaws.

'Gah!' cried Leonora.

'Squark!' cried Twitchy.

'Wow!' cried Jack.

As they backed away, they heard a sickening **TAPATAPTAPTATTPATPAT** sound behind them. They spun round. Inside the pod, thousands of winged insects with hairy legs were crawling around. At the centre of the pod was a scientist covered in the super-creepy-crawlies, calmly writing notes.

'No way – those look like spider wasps,' said Jack. 'That must be a totally new species!'

'I hate this place,' groaned Leonora.

'*Squooooook*,' agreed Twitchy.

'And, look,' said Jack, 'this must be where they created the Dromad we used to cross the Perilous Desert.' He pointed to the next pod where a lifelike robot camel was standing on a sand dune. 'Whoa, I'd love to work with the animals in here.'

'I'm afraid it takes years to get a job in the bureau,' came a sharp voice behind them. A young woman approached. She had hair like Medusa in the morning and similar levels of charm. 'Come along, we haven't much time.'

'Who are you?' asked Leonora.

'None of your business,' the woman replied.

'Bit rude,' muttered Jack.

'No, I can't reveal my name,' she explained. 'You can call me Boffin One. I'm taking you to our most secret department to select your bad gadget. Let's go.'

Leonora, Twitchy and Jack followed the mysterious woman further into the cavern. Each pod they passed was more bizarre than the last. In one room, black snow flurried down from the ceiling, forming menacing drifts. In another, sabre-toothed corgis wandered in and out of kennels on stubby legs. They passed what looked like a swaying field of wheat, but on closer inspection Leonora could see that the stalks had faces and . . . what were those? *Teeth.*

'This way,' said the woman. 'And stay close.'

Leonora, Jack and Twitchy practically glued themselves to her side as they reached a door with DEPARTMENT OF WHOOPS written on it. Yet

more codes, twelve different sets of keys and full-body laser scans were required before the door eventually opened. And they stepped into . . . the bizarre heart of SIG.

15

The Department of Whoops

'Um . . . what *is* this place?' asked Leonora, scratching her head. Jack and Twitchy exchanged baffled looks. They'd stepped inside a glorious rose garden, complete with thatched country cottage and a view of rolling meadows stretching off into the distance. The sky was cornflower blue. Insects buzzed lazily about the rose bushes and honeysuckle.

'It's a simulation,' said Boffin One, 'a testing zone where we carry out some unusual experiments using dangerous technology. You'd better keep your wits about you.' The door slammed shut behind them like a lid falling on a coffin.

'Doesn't exactly *look* dangerous,' whispered Jack, as they walked along a stone path and over a dainty bridge. Twitchy's whiskers bristled as he eyed the hopping bunnies and waddling ducklings all around them.

'Things are not always what they seem,' replied Boffin One, as they passed the cottage and moved on into daisy-dotted fields beyond.

'Maybe you can be injured from cuteness overload?' whispered Leonora, gazing about at the blissful scene.

'Yeah, death by fluffiness,' said Jack. 'Terrible way to go.'

But as he said this, they heard a faint **FLARPING** and **YELPING** sound like beagles playing bugles. Two scientists wearing white coats and crash helmets hurdled over a wall in the distance and dashed down the hill towards them. In the sky just behind their heads, a strange dark cloud appeared.

'It's OK. I – I think they're just starlings,' said Jack. 'When they fly in formation like that it's called a murmuration.' He gave Leonora a proud nod. Twitchy growled and bared his teeth. The scientists sped up and started to scream.

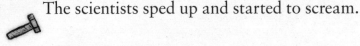

'I'm afraid those aren't birds,' said Boffin One, backing away. 'They're flying **Robo-Hamsters**. I told the team not to let them out!' She ushered them all behind a nearby cherry tree.

'Wow, *cool*!' cried Jack, watching in amazement as the flock approached.

'Maybe I could use them for the games,' agreed Leonora, sneaking a look at the creatures round the tree trunk.

'Sure!' shouted Boffin One, over the rising sound of squeaks. 'You can take a couple, but they're tricky to catch.' By now, the rodents had reached the scientists and started dive-bombing their heads.

'Jack, got any hamster facts that could help us?' asked Leonora.

'Well . . . they eat their own poop.'

'Urgh, gross. Anything else?'

'My hamster, Hammy, doesn't like getting wet.'

Leonora frowned, but then remembered something. She fumbled in her tool belt and pulled out her Christmas present from Jack. 'Here, take this!'

Jack nodded as she handed him the mini fire extinguisher. He took a deep breath and emerged from behind the tree, keeping low to the ground. As he approached the flock, he lifted the nozzle and sprayed a jet of water into the air ahead of him. A couple of the robots got drenched, squealed and fell down. He gently scooped them up and sprinted back.

'Nice one!' cried Leonora.

'Yes, expertly done,' said Boffin One, as a rumble filled the air. 'And not a moment too soon!'

'What's that noise?' asked Jack.

'A random earthquake generator.' She gestured towards the stream, which was now glowing neon orange. 'And it looks like they're also just about to begin the everything-is-lava simulation – let's go!'

Leonora took the disarmed hamsters and tucked them inside her tool belt. Jack scooped up Twitchy as the grass began to really (really) heat up. And they both sprinted after Boffin One back towards the exit, leaping through the door just as the charming countryside behind them went full-on Pompeii. Zone 13 had turned into a raging volcanic storm.

Back in the nothing-is-lava safety of Zone 1, Leonora and Jack were in the lab, tinkering with dismantled robot rodents.

'I'm just not sure how to make Robo-Hamsters scary or gross,' said Leonora. 'They need to be *really* bad.'

'Don't worry, I've got loads of facts that could help,' said Jack. 'Like hamster teeth never stop growing, which is weird. And they can store loads of stuff in their cheeks.'

'OK, cool, we can use that,' said Leonora, grabbing a set of screwdrivers.

Jack gave her a lopsided grin. 'And I've got an idea to make them *really* awful.' He drew a quick sketch.

'*Wow*,' said Leonora, 'that's terrible – let's go for it!'

As they worked together to make adjustments, **SQUILCH**, **FNORP** and **RAT-A-TAT** noises echoed round the lab. A whiff of scorched fake fur filled the air. Twitchy sat on the table beside them, nudging tools over with his nose. It took a couple of hours, but at last the bad hamsters were ready!

'Excellent work,' said Professor Puri, joining them in the lab and inspecting the robots. 'I can see that you've done your very worst. Let's just hope this secures your place in the final. Everything is riding on it.'

For several nerve-racking minutes, Leonora and Jack watched as Professor Puri entered their invention into the Great Gadget Games website. She even added a video of the hamsters in action, fatally injuring a tea towel.

'Is there any news about the Captain?' Leonora asked, as Mildred arrived moments later, clutching the **Captain Spang Monitor** device. 'Has he found HMS *Invisible* – and the answer to the 313 riddle?'

Mildred shook her head. 'I've been monitoring closely but the signal has dropped out,' she said. 'He's gone and got himself lost in the Ominous Ocean, the silly old fool! I should never have let him go.'

Leonora felt her throat tighten. She hurried over and gave Mildred a hug. 'He'll find his way back to us, Millie,' she whispered. 'I know he will.'

Just then, Professor Puri's laptop made a pinging noise. A new message appeared on screen:

**Congratulations,
Lenny Cornflake!
You win our wild-card place.**

Please proceed to Studio 9, Bleakly Road, Greydon, on 31 December at 4 p.m.

'Wow, I can't believe we did it,' said Leonora, letting go of Mildred. She stared at the screen, feeling a fresh spark of determination.

This was it. The final furlong, the last lap – victory was in sight! She was going to get to the studio, rescue her parents and bring her uncle's terrible plans crashing down around him. Everything was going to run as smoothly as buttered clockwork.

16

Showtime

It was New Year's Eve but there wasn't a party popper in sight. Instead, Leonora was standing in the fading light outside an enormous bleak industrial estate. Before her she could see dozens of guards patrolling fences topped with barbed wire and spikes.

'Am I really going in *there*?'

'I'm afraid you are,' whispered Brenda, who was disguised as a lamp post beside her. 'Luther's clearly beefed up his security.'

No kidding, thought Leonora. It looked more like a high-security prison than a glamorous TV studio.

'I'm afraid we were unable to intercept your parents,' Brenda continued, 'so they must be inside. But I've upgraded Jack's hoodie disguise, which hopefully means he and Twitchy will have managed to sneak in among the TV audience by now. You won't be alone.'

Despite Brenda's reassurances, Leonora felt fear tiptoe down her spine, then stomp back up in hobnail boots. She patted her tool belt where one of the **Robo-Hamsters** was safely hidden. And the Identigo had called a truce and wasn't trying to turn her into pineapple chunks or a potty either. It was now or never.

'Remember,' said Brenda, 'when it's your turn to showcase your invention, try to create a diversion. Jack will give you a nod when it's time. That should allow our SIG operatives to get through security and rescue you all. Good luck!'

'Thanks,' Leonora replied. 'I think I'm going to need it.'

Leonora walked slowly along the road towards the studio gates. As she approached, security guards immediately appeared and blocked her way. 'No entry!' bellowed one through a loudhailer.

'Hi! Um, I'm – I'm Lenny Cornflake,' she replied, 'the wild-card winner? I'm due in the studio.'

The man scowled and checked his notes. 'Ah yes, you're just in time,' he said with a smirk. 'In you go.'

Leonora was led past the main gates and through five sets of steel doors. Each one was locked behind her, as if she was being trapped inside a puzzle box. They then had to navigate a maze and cross a large moat before they finally arrived at the main studio building. *I'll never find my way back out!* she thought.

'Off you pop then,' said another one of the guards, as Leonora stepped from the rubber dinghy. She was met by a hassled-looking studio manager with a blonde ponytail.

'Welcome to the games,' she said in the least welcoming voice ever. 'You're late. We need you backstage for hair and make-up right now. We're live in ten minutes.'

Leonora felt a jab of panic. *My disguise!* 'I – I definitely don't need make-up,' she said quickly. 'I, er – I've already got that on.'

'Fine, whatever. Let's go.' The woman flicked her hair and strode off.

Leonora jogged to keep up. She followed her ever deeper into the complex, before they eventually stepped into a large backstage green room. Through an adjoining window Leonora could see a massive studio filled with camera people, lighting technicians and floor managers. The audience was filing in. Had Jack made it through?

'Ha, if it isn't Little Flake, I mean *Corn*flake.' Leonora spun round and came face to face with Bonald. 'Didn't think you'd made the grade,' he said with a sneer.

'I'm the wild card,' Leonora replied, willing her voice not to wobble. She looked around the room. Nine other kids were waiting nervously for the show to begin, each standing beside a strange-looking contraption. Leonora was relieved to see Jian, Scarlett and Meera. They smiled and waved at her.

'Well, *I'm* going to take that top prize,' said Bonald. 'My invention is totally wicked!'

'I'm sure it is,' said Leonora. 'First the *worst*.'

Bonald stepped forward to give her a shove, but just then a door at the back of the room swung open. All the candidates turned round.

There were claps and giggles of delight as Barry Tremendous strode into the room. And behind him marched six enormous bodyguards who stepped aside to reveal . . .

Leonora's jaw dropped to the floor. Her heart very nearly cannonballed out of her chest. Huddled together were two people that she'd almost lost hope of ever seeing again. A halo of bright light seemed to gleam all around them.

Time expanded – stars exploded – angels wept. It was her mum and dad.

17
Family Misfortunes

'No way,' Leonora whispered, eyes ablaze. It took every single ounce of her willpower not to leap across the room right there and then – and shriek, weep and hug her parents silly! Instead, she dug her fingernails into her palms. *Not now. Be patient.*

'Attention, contestants!' cried Barry. 'I'd like you all to meet our terrific guest judges, Eliza and Harry Bolt. They're going to be picking our winner shortly.'

Leonora stared at them. Her mum's expression was one of steel; she held her head high. Her dad looked uneasy – his arm circled Eliza's shoulders.

For a brief moment their gaze landed on Leonora. She felt as if her heart would burst into flames, like a Viking longship on its voyage to heaven. *Mum, Dad – it's me, it's me!* she screamed inside. But they looked away again without recognizing her.

'Now, contestants, collect your things and come with me,' said Barry. 'The world is waiting for your bad gadgets and, more importantly, so is Lord Luther.' With that, he turned and swept out of the room.

The guards jostled Harry and Eliza behind him. The other children picked up their devices and excitedly followed the grown-ups out of the door, with Leonora pushed to the back. They were led into the huge TV studio with a stage decorated like an Olympic arena. Three golden Gs were suspended from the rigging above. The jewel-encrusted Uncle Luther trophy sparkled on a massive stand. Leonora watched as her mum and dad were shoved towards two red thrones at the back of the set. Cameras tracked forwards and backwards while dance music pumped in the background.

'Take your places,' said the studio manager, leading the kids to a semicircle of podiums centre stage. The music went quiet. 'We're live in three – two – one.'

'Goooooood evening, everyone!' Barry jumped on to the stage to frantic applause. He grinned and shot finger guns in the direction of Eliza and Harry. 'Welcome, everyone, to the grand final of the Great Gadget Games! Let's bring back to the stage the man, the genius, *the inventing legend*, Lord Luther Brightspark!'

The audience went completely wild as a third throne was slowly lowered from the rigging and set down between Leonora's parents. Uncle Luther was perched on it dressed like an emperor, wearing a purple cloak and a wonky crown of golden leaves. He didn't say a word, only grimaced and waved to his fans.

Leonora tried to ignore the uproar. Her eyes scanned the studio for escape routes. A guard was positioned at each of the two exits. And there was no sign of Jack and Twitchy. Panic pricked her like an irritable cactus. Her fingertips felt inside her pocket. Would the hamsters be bad enough to save them all?

'Without further ado,' said Barry, 'let's begin our gadget battle! Contestant number one at the ready!'

Leonora watched as a little boy at the far end of the semicircle was ushered to the centre of the stage. He placed a cardboard crate on the floor and looked towards Uncle Luther, who made a regal gesture for him to continue.

'H-hi, um, my name's Jamie,' he stammered, 'and my invention is a Weather Warper.' He lifted the lid and a fluffy white cloud escaped, hovering just above the ground.

'It's got loads of settings,' he said, twiddling a remote control. The cloud rumbled, turned grey and expanded to the size of a bus. There was a flash of lightning. It began to rain ice cubes on to the stage.

'And watch this!' Jamie turned a dial several more times to create a deluge of snotty tissues, sticky weeds, drawing pins, rotten eggs and, finally, toenails. There were gasps and *urghs* from the audience.

'Totally splendido!' cried Barry. 'I'm sure Lord Luther could use a brain like yours at Brightspark Industries.' He glanced up at the thrones. Uncle Luther slowly raised his thumb in agreement, then shot a twisted smile at the stony-faced Harry and Eliza.

'Great! Let's have our next contestant,' said Barry.

One by one the children showcased their ghastly gadgets. Bonald demonstrated a Go-Gossip listening device for spying on your friends. A little girl unveiled her Traffic Jam, to be spread on motorways and cause travel misery.

And a teenage boy revealed a NitWit band, a bracelet to erase the wearer's sense of danger.

As time ticked by, Leonora felt her head start to spin. Just one of these technologies could cause global mayhem. The show *mustn't* go on – Uncle Luther had to be stopped! She stole a quick glance towards the thrones. He looked dangerously calm, while her parents' expressions were now worried.

'We'll be right back after these adverts. Don't go away!' said Barry as they cut to a break. The lights came on and Leonora was able to see into the audience at last. To her relief she spied Jack three rows back, slumped down in his seat and with an otter-shaped lump under his hoodie. He gave her a covert wave. This was her moment!

'*Psst*,' she whispered to Scarlett, who was standing on the next podium over.

While she'd got Scarlett's attention, Leonora scribbled a note, screwed it into a ball and chucked it over to her. Scarlett caught it and uncrumpled the note:

Luther Brightspark is actually my horrible uncle. Eliza and Harry are my parents – and his prisoners! Please help me save them!

Scarlett frowned and looked over. Leonora pressed her palms together and pleaded with wide eyes. There was a desperate pause, but then Scarlett nodded and passed the message along the line. Jian, Meera and the other kids read it in turn, although when it reached Bonald his hand shot up – he was going to snitch! But, just in the nick of time –

'Positions, everyone!' said the manager as the studio lights dimmed. 'We're live again in five, four, three, two – one!'

As the cameras started rolling once more, Leonora sprang into action. 'NOW!' she cried, running to the middle of the stage. All the contestants (except Bonald) jumped out from behind their podiums and gathered round her. With mischievous grins they let loose their gadgets and machines.

TOTAL CHAOS!

Mushy peas and curry sauce poured down on to the stage all around them. A Vacuum De-Cleaner belched out great clouds of carpet dust. Scarlett's Shriek Machine played hideous screams and whelps, while Meera's Snot Cannon shot out globs of gross gloop. The kids aimed their inventions at each of the guards in turn, before unleashing them on Bonald!

'That's so not fair!' he whined, trying to rub off the layers of slime now covering him. 'I should be the winner!'

'Bullies never win!' shouted Meera, giving Scarlett a fist bump.

By now, members of the audience were leaping from their seats and racing towards the exits. A weird smell, like sparklers and boiled turnips, filled the air.

'Robo-attack!' Leonora shouted above the mayhem. She pulled out her hamster, clicked its power button and aimed it at the thrones behind her. Jack jumped up on his chair and did the same. The rodents flew high across the studio and straight to their target. But when they reached Uncle Luther, they circled his head – then flew right through him!

'What the . . . ? *Nooooooo!*' Leonora cried, feeling her stomach drop like a broken yo-yo.

'What's wrong?' shouted Jian.

'It's a trick! My uncle – he's just a hologram!'

Sure enough, they watched the hamsters swoop several more times through his ghostly body before the image flickered off. Meanwhile, two of Luther's henchmen had seized Eliza and Harry and were hauling them towards the back of the stage.

'Leo, run!' shouted Jack as he scrabbled over the seats towards her. 'I'm right behind you!'

'Yes, go!' cried Jian. 'Save your parents! We'll keep the guards busy!'

Leonora grabbed the belt from round her waist and ripped off the Identigo, returning to her true appearance. She then ran as fast as she could through the mess, dust and confusion – hot on the heels of her mum and dad. A single thought blazed in her brain: *I won't lose you this time!*

18

Backstage Passes

'Mum, Dad!' Leonora screamed as the dust cleared.

'Leonora!' came the weak reply.

She spun to her right. Her parents were being marched through the fast-collapsing stage set. Leonora sprinted after them, dodging falling lights and fake marble columns. She raced out of the studio and through a labyrinth of backstage corridors. 'I'm coming!' she yelled, pushing her way through heavy doors, her heart pounding, lungs aching. Every time she thought she was catching up, they turned another corner and were just out of reach.

At one point Harry cried over his shoulder, 'Leo, we love you!'

'I love you too!' she shouted, running even faster, tears blurring her eyes.

At last she turned down another long hallway lined with windows. Leonora let out a cry. Right at the end, just thirty feet away, she was amazed, astonished and ecstatic to see –

'Mum! Is that . . . *you*?' Leonora rubbed her face, blinking hard.

Eliza turned round.

In that blissful moment Leonora felt as if the world around her had completely fallen away. The clocks had stopped. The universe had shrunk to a single point of light. She stared at her mum, as clear as day, as real as can be.

Eliza covered her mouth with her palms and swayed slightly. She started walking and then running towards Leonora. She held her arms out wide.

Leonora raced towards her! But just as she was about to be swept into her mother's embrace after all this time, Leonora noticed that something didn't look right. At the very edges of her mum's face, so faint that you could barely see it, she could just make out . . . a pale blueish tinge.

'NOOOOOO!' Leonora screamed, falling backwards.

'Yes indeed!' came a booming voice. Before Leonora's horrified eyes, Eliza's face changed, her body stretched and she transformed into . . . Uncle Luther!

Leonora's heels slipped on the floor as she tried to back away. Luther was now standing right over her, his face twisted with victory.

'Marvellous bit of kit,' he said, pointing to the device on his belt that looked exactly like an **Identigo**. 'You really must thank the SIG team for me.'

'But – but how did *you* get hold of it?'

'I *knew* there was something funny about you, Lenny Cornflake,' he said with a sneer, 'so, out in the forest, I had extra cameras trained on you non-stop! When you recharged your batteries, I took close-up pictures of your disguise device. I then had your parents copy the technology in record time! It seems they still have their uses.'

'But Mum, Dad . . . where are they?' she sobbed.

'Oh, don't worry about them. They're being escorted by my men to a newly built laboratory up in the mountains.'

As he said this, Leonora heard the thrumming of an engine outside. Behind her uncle, through a window to her right, she glimpsed a black quadcopter parked in the centre of a courtyard. She could just see her mother inside it with two guards either side of her on the back seat. They had cross expressions.

'But that's not where you're going, my silly little mess. I have other plans for you.'

'I'm not going *anywhere* with you!' she shouted, white-hot anger flashing through her like lightning.

'That's a pity. We make such a great team, you and I.' Uncle Luther paused, passing a trembling hand across his brow. He removed his crooked crown and let it drop to the floor with a *clang*.

'I can never be happy, Leonora – I realize that now – but *you* could. Why don't you join *me*? The world could be your oyster! You could live with your parents, be my heir and eventually take over Brightspark Industries!'

For the teeniest, tiniest moment, Leonora felt the terrible tug of temptation, like a rip current pulling her underwater. All the struggle, all the fight would be over. She'd finally have what she'd always craved. Her family would be complete. *She* would be complete. But then she remembered the bad gadgets, the misery and mayhem, the forces of chaos.

'I'd rather *die* than work with you!' She spat the words out.

'Fine! Then you can work *for* me instead!' He lunged forward and grabbed her.

She squirmed and twisted to get free from his bony clutches. But just as he was dragging her kicking and screaming towards the exit, something unexpected started to happen. Just a few feet behind them, a snack machine started to make some unusual **ZIZZING** noises. All the chocolate bars, cola cans and crisps started to shimmy and shake, as if performing the samba. And before their very eyes, it bent out of shape and shrank rapidly, turning into –

'DAD!'

Harry Bolt dived towards them. 'LEO!' he cried, grabbing Leonora's free hand. 'Get away from her, you monster!'

For a few seconds there was a horrible tug of war as she was pulled between the two of them. But, just at that moment, Jack and Twitchy burst through a door at the other end of the corridor. Jack was holding his **Sure-Shot** football.

'Leo, duck!' He kicked the ball hard and it soared through the air into Uncle Luther's stomach, knocking him to the ground.

Harry grabbed Leonora and swept her up into his arms.

'He shoots – he scores!' cried Jack.

'SQUOOK!' squarked Twitchy, who was

carrying the two **Robo-Hamsters** on his back. He flicked them up into the air, and they too flew straight towards their target.

'Urgh, disgusting!' Uncle Luther cried, as the hamsters circled him and began a pooping frenzy. Stinking brown pellets rained down on him like bullets. Flames shot out of their mouths, setting his wig and moustache alight. He jumped up on his gangly legs, desperately swatting them away. 'You'll pay for this, Leonora!' he screeched, before realizing that a camera woman had arrived on the scene and was broadcasting the entire incident live to the world.

He looked aghast, and tried to shield his face. 'No, no, dear fans – this – this isn't the real me! There's been some sort of mistaaaaake!' He turned on his heels and dashed away.

'Leo, that was *epic*!' cried Jack, sliding to a halt in front of her and giving her a double high-five.

'*You* were epic!' she cried. 'But we can't let him escape; he's still got Mum!'

'He won't get away this time!' shouted Harry, placing Leonora down. He raced after Luther as he disappeared round the corner.

'Go, Dad – faster!' screamed Leonora, running behind them into the next hallway.

Just as they were both about to catch up with him, Uncle Luther slipped through the only door into the courtyard. He pushed a big red button on the other side and the door slammed shut behind him, locking itself tight.

'No, no, no!' cried Leonora, looking through a window, as Uncle Luther raced towards the quadcopter, clutching his keys. She and Harry thumped and kicked the door with all their might, but it wouldn't budge. 'Mum!'

Leonora stepped sideways and tried to break through the window instead. Her palms stung as she slapped them against the cold glass.

Across the courtyard, Eliza reached out to press her hand against the quadcopter's window, but the guards stopped her.

'Mum – I'll find you, I'll *never give up*!' Leonora cried.

Uncle Luther had unlocked the pilot's door and jumped in. Rotor blades whipped wind about the courtyard. The quadcopter rose up, up and away into the cold night sky. In seconds its lights had faded to nothing . . . It was gone.

'Leo . . . my little bean . . . it's OK,' came a soft voice behind her.

Leonora felt strong arms circling her and lifting her off the ground again. She turned her head and buried her face in her dad's shoulder. A thousand feelings crashed over her all at once. She was sobbing with frustration and anger, but also with joy.

19
Father's Day

'Dad . . . Daddy . . . *Daaadeee*. Time to get up,' whispered Leonora, pushing a finger up her father's unsuspecting nostril.

'Huh, Leo – where are you?' cried Harry, waking up with a start. He blinked, his eyes darting around the room. Then –

'I can't believe it's really you, my little bean,' he said, pulling Leonora up on to his hospital bed and hugging her tight.

It was New Year's Day. The dawn of another year. A fresh page, a new chapter. Leonora, Twitchy, Jack and Harry were in SIG's medical rooms. Under Professor Puri's orders, Harry had been kept in overnight. Leonora had insisted on staying too, squooshed up in the next bed with Jack and Twitchy. Unable to sleep, she'd spent the whole night gazing at her dad, mostly resisting the urge to poke him and confirm that he was real.

'Here we are, me dearest Harry!' cried Mildred, bustling on to the ward moments later. She was clutching a plate groaning with eggs, bacon and green pudding. 'Just a little breakfast treat; you'll be needing your strength back!'

Harry beamed at Mildred. 'Smells delicious, Professor D.'

'Go on with you. I'm not your tutor now,' she said, grinning back. 'It's Millie to you.'

'Millie, I can't –' Harry took a deep breath and tried again. 'I can't thank you enough for keeping Leo safe all this time.'

Mildred nodded, then burst into tears. That set them all off. Before long, a chorus of happy sobs echoed around the ward. Twitchy squooked and bounced about the bed.

'I can't believe you're really back,' said Leonora at last, wiping her face. 'But Mum's still out there, still a prisoner.'

'Yeah, and Luther's got away *again*,' said Jack, frowning.

Harry's face fell. 'Our plan was for both of us to escape,' he said, 'but we agreed that if only one of us could, we should just go for it. So we secretly created *two* Identigos. We gave one to Luther but kept the other for ourselves. As we were bundled out of the building towards the quadcopter, Eliza distracted the guard who was fastening her seat belt, and grabbed his key fob –'

'Go, Mum!' Leonora interrupted, punching the air in delight.

'Indeed! She threw the key to me, and I pushed the other guard into the quad, shutting the door and locking them all inside. I hated to leave your mum behind, but she gave me a nod, and I knew I had to do it so I could help you stop Luther. That gave me the chance to run back into the building and change into the vending machine. But it seems Luther had his own key and was still able to get away.'

'Whoa, impressive teamwork,' said Jack. 'But . . . what's it been like? Not being a snack machine – being a hostage, I mean.'

'We were moved around a lot and kept in very basic living quarters –' Harry wrinkled his nose – 'and the food, well, that was the worst you've ever tasted.'

Leonora eyed Mildred and elbowed Jack before he could open his mouth. Harry continued:

'The engineering work Luther made us complete on his awful schemes was a distraction from the pain of missing you, Leo, but he couldn't understand why we were so heartbroken. He just doesn't experience happiness . . . or love.'

Leonora nodded, remembering how broken her uncle had looked. 'I think he's given up on trying to be happy. He just wants everyone else to be miserable too,' she said. 'He's more dangerous than ever. We've got to rescue Mum!'

'We will, no matter what,' said Harry, smoothing her hair. 'I *swear* it.'

'We'll get Angus back too,' said Mildred.

Harry frowned. 'Who's Angus?'

'Captain Angus Spang is my other guardian, and Millie's husband,' said Leonora. 'He's the best and also the worst sailor in the world!'

'Looks like he's done us proud,' said Mildred. 'I've traced him as far as the South Swiss Seas and think he's found HMS *Invisible*. I should make radio contact with him later today.'

'Excellent work, Professor Dribble,' said Professor Insignia, who'd just arrived on to the ward.

'Yes, that's great news,' said Harry, 'because

we need that boat back as soon as possible. Is it safe for me to discuss what's on board?'

Professor Insignia paused, glanced at Leonora and then nodded.

'When we were kidnapped by Luther in the Arctic Circle all those years ago, we were conducting top-secret scientific research. Our notes are hidden in locker number 313 on board HMS *Invisible*.'

'That's the number you left us as a clue around BrightWorld!' Leonora cried.

'Yes. We couldn't tell you the meaning in case Luther or one of his cronies figured it out. Inside that locker is our research material. It refers to something out in the Antarctic wilderness.'

'Don't you mean the Arctic?' Leonora frowned. 'That's where you were snatched?'

'Actually, no, the phrase "a world turned upside down" meant the *opposite* pole. Again, we were trying to throw Luther off the scent with our riddles.'

'Ahhh,' chorused Leonora and Jack, grinning at the discovery.

'What have you found?' said Professor Insignia. 'Can you tell us more?'

Harry sighed, rubbed his forehead with his wrist. 'In Dyrne Library we stumbled upon some scientific diaries written over a hundred

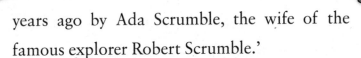

years ago by Ada Scrumble, the wife of the famous explorer Robert Scrumble.'

'Oh, I think I remembers their work,' said Mildred, looking thoughtful. 'She was the brains of the operation; he was the big flappy mouth.'

'OK . . . but what did they discover?' asked Leonora.

'They sailed the world, searching for remote tribes,' Harry replied. 'Ada studied the early inventions of ancient people and human behaviour. She also discovered a strange force field and weird tremors in the Antarctic. We used the diaries from Dyrne College to follow their research on our trip aboard HMS *Invisible*. It's been so long since I read them that I can't remember more. But I do know they mustn't fall into the wrong hands.'

'Yeah,' said Jack, 'like Luther's.'

Leonora bit her lip. She thought about how close her uncle had come to fulfilling his latest wicked scheme and unleashing all those bad gadgets on the world. 'So what happened to all the horrible inventions from the games?'

'They've been safely delivered to the Department of Whoops so that we can study them,' said Professor Insignia. 'There's no such thing as evil technology, but it's SIG's job to ensure humans use it for good.'

'Well, that's a bloomin' relief,' said Mildred. 'We can't have it raining cowpats or whatever.'

'Quite so,' agreed Professor Insignia.

'And what about the diamond-encrusted Luther trophy?' asked Leonora. 'I know someone with a big family who could use it . . .' She side-eyed Jack. He blushed and shook his head.

'I couldn't do that,' he mumbled.

'We do need to find a use for it,' said Professor Insignia, 'although there's something else that I'd like to discuss first.' He looked a little awkward and cleared his throat. 'Leonora

. . . I would like to invite you to join us here at SIG alongside your father. You have proved yourself the most extraordinary inventor and leader. Your teamwork and ingenuity have shone brightly once again.'

Leonora felt her cheeks burn. 'But . . . I thought you said that SIG was no place for children?'

'I'll admit . . . I got that wrong,' he said. 'I was trying to protect you, but I can see that you're more than capable of taking care of yourself, and others. And the games reminded me that children's imaginations are limitless. It's just that sort of thinking that we need here at SIG.'

'Yeah,' agreed Leonora, 'and I made some cool new friends too; they could be the future of the society!'

'It's like I've been trying to tell you,' said Jack, 'grown-ups need to think more like kids. We're much brainier.' He gave Leonora an affectionate jab in the ribs. Twitchy squarked and rubbed his wet nose against her legs.

'So what do you say?' asked Professor Insignia.

'I say yes!' cried Leonora, a bubble of joy bursting inside her.

At that moment Professor Puri entered the room. 'Our dear, secret inventor, Leonora

Bolt,' she said, 'and Professor Harry Bolt, I'm delighted to say that these are for you.'

Professor Puri handed Leonora a parcel. She stared at it before tearing the brown paper apart. Inside were two starched white laboratory coats, each with a golden spanner pin on the lapel. In fancy embroidery were stitched the words:

'You've earned your rightful place here,' continued Professor Insignia, giving Leonora a formal handshake. 'And we have many challenges ahead. We must protect the world from people like Luther, who use good technology in bad ways. Welcome to the society, ingenious genius. The sky's the limit.'

Leonora felt as if she might actually start

floating. 'This is brilliant, thank you,' she said at last. 'But Jack and Twitch need to join too! I can't work without them.'

'You can't?' asked Jack.

'Definitely not!' she replied. 'You two bring the animal magic.'

Jack gave her a proud look. 'Yeah, maybe . . . I could set up SIG's awesome animal academy. I could use the money from selling the Luther trophy to help protect amazing creatures and learn from them.'

Professor Insignia snapped his fingers. 'That is an excellent suggestion, young man. We need your passion and skills here at the society too. Welcome.'

Jack let out a '**WOO-HOO!**' and Twitchy did a forward roll and squarked with joy.

Leonora felt herself grinning from ear to ear. Everyone beamed back at her. But the widest smile came from her dad. It was a smile that looked exactly like hers. She tried to speak but the words got stuck in her throat. So instead she just allowed the feeling of warmth and happiness to spread through her.

She'd finally earned her place at SIG, and with her best friends too. And her family was nearly complete. Leonora had never felt more confident and capable. Nothing was going to stand in her way again!

She took out her notebook and pencil and revised her to-do list:

Save Mum.
Save the world.
Get Dad to trim his nostril hair.

Right at this moment there wasn't a scrap of doubt in her mind that she could do it. This was a new dawn, a new day – time for her to write a new story. *I'm a SIG inventor. The very best in the world. Nothing is impossible if I use my imagination.*

THE END

(Is it? Maybe not.)

Otterly Thankful

What an otter privilege it is to have four Leonora Bolt books out in the world! Twitchy Nibbles has asked if he can say a few words of thanks this time. I hope I've understood him properly as Otterish can be tricky to translate. Here goes . . .

A grateful squark and shiny pebbles to the incredible Puffin team, especially editor extraordinaire Katie Sinfield. A huge tail wag to amazing editorial manager Josh Benn and awesome designers Andrea Kearney, Nigel Baines and Ben Hughes. A special roly-poly for PR and marketing legends Charlotte Winstone, Mhari Nimmo and Cara Evans.

To the fantastically talented Gladys Jose and the Artful Doodlers, Twitchy sends his mightiest paw squeeze. He says you've captured his (super cute) whiskers perfectly!

Massive squeals and a performance of rock juggling to fabulous agents Elizabeth Counsell and Hannah Weatherill, as well as Natalie Christopher and the Northbank Talent team.

To all the Leonora readers, Twitchy sends huge thanks and ear scritches. He says you can all play on his favourite muddy bank. And he gives squeals of gratitude to the amazing 2022 author gang, and to Meng Wang.

But Twitchy reserves his biggest nose-boops and herring burps for C, M and W. Lucky you! x

**Discover where it
all began, with book 1
of the otterly brilliant
Leonora Bolt series . . .**

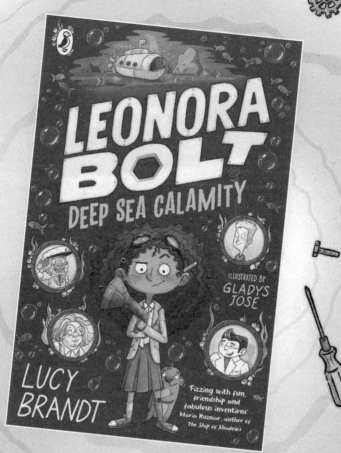

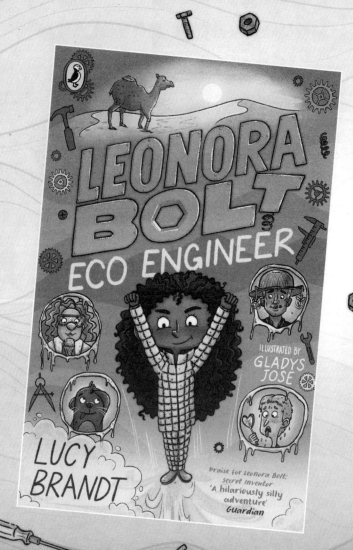